Fiona Rich lived in St Andrews, Fife, as a teenager before moving to Edinburgh, then on to Birmingham to commence her nurse training. Moving into nurse education after a span in clinical practice, she spent 25 years as a senior university lecturer, specialising in learning disability nursing and epilepsy care.

Now retired, as well as finding a new passion for creative writing, she enjoys spending time playing tennis and walking in the Highlands of Scotland.

She has been married for 36 years and has two adult children.

*To Linda*
*with many thanks*
*Fiona Rich*
*x.*
*Enjoy!*

This book is dedicated to my dad, who, during his professional life as a student counsellor both at the University of St Andrews and the University of Dundee, supported many students. I recall when he retired a number of years ago, a conversation we had where he told me that there needed to be more support for young men with psychological traumas because they tended to be less willing to come to counselling and ended up with more psychological problems as a result.

This conversation stayed with me and was the catalyst for my characters Tim and Josh. Without that conversation, this book would not have been written.

Thank you, Nick, for your constant guidance and inspiration.

**Fiona Rich**

# A Story to Tell; A Secret to Keep

**Austin Macauley Publishers**
LONDON · CAMBRIDGE · NEW YORK · SHARJAH

Copyright © Fiona Rich 2023

The right of Fiona Rich to be identified as author of this work has been asserted by the author in accordance with sections 77 and 78 of the Copyright, Designs and Patents Act 1988.

All rights reserved. No part of this publication may be reproduced, stored in a retrieval system, or transmitted in any form or by any means, electronic, mechanical, photocopying, recording, or otherwise, without the prior permission of the publishers.

Any person who commits any unauthorised act in relation to this publication may be liable to criminal prosecution and civil claims for damages.

This is a work of fiction. Names, characters, businesses, places, events, locales, and incidents are either the products of the author's imagination or used in a fictitious manner. Any resemblance to actual persons, living or dead, or actual events is purely coincidental.

A CIP catalogue record for this title is available from the British Library.

ISBN 9781398494794 (Paperback)
ISBN 9781398494800 (ePub e-book)

www.austinmacauley.com

First Published 2023
Austin Macauley Publishers Ltd®
1 Canada Square
Canary Wharf
London
E14 5AA

When I said to my husband, Stuart, one day in lockdown, "Do you think I could write a novel?" his immediate response was, "Yes, of course you could."

Thank you, Stuart, for always believing in me and for supporting me in every challenge I give myself.

There is a tiny art café in Kincraig called the Old Post Office Café Gallery that we go to whenever we are in the Highlands. They do indeed sell amazing coffee, cakes and focaccia and often have a '70s' vibe playlist. (It is well worth a visit – you won't be disappointed!) One day when I was sitting in the café listening to the very song that I cited in the novel, I imagined the character Josh and his father sitting there having a conversation – low and behold, it became part of the storyline. Thank you, Toni and Ann, for the inspiration and for the cakes!

Thank you to my proofreaders, Alex, Åsa, Helen, Marie, Natalie, Nick and Samantha, for your feedback and encouragement. Thank you also to Mandy for your insight into a banking career for women in the 1980s and 1990s.

# Table of Contents

**Prologue** — **11**

**Part 1** — **15**

   1: Libby – Edinburgh, 1983 — 17

   2: Tim – Edinburgh, 1983 — 31

   3: Libby – Edinburgh, 1983 — 39

   4: Tim – Edinburgh, 1983 — 51

**Part 2** — **61**

   5: Libby – Cupar, August, 1983 — 63

   6: Libby – Edinburgh, October, 1983 — 74

   7: Tim – Edinburgh, June, 1984 — 79

   8: Tim – Boarding School, 1975 — 85

   9: Libby – September, 1988 — 96

   11: Libby – Birmingham, September, 1988 — 113

**Part 3** — **119**

   12: Libby – Sandstone Manor, December, 1990 — 121

   13: Libby – Birmingham, September, 1998 — 128

| | |
|---|---|
| 14: Tim – Birmingham, September, 1998 | 132 |
| 15: Libby – Birmingham, April, 2009 | 135 |
| 16: Tim – Birmingham, April, 2009 | 140 |
| 17: Josh – Birmingham, May, 2009 | 143 |
| 18: Josh – Manchester, September, 2011 | 152 |
| 19: Libby – Birmingham, December, 2012 | 158 |
| 20: Tim – Birmingham, December, 2012 | 163 |
| **Part 4** | **165** |
| 21: Tim – Edinburgh, January, 2013 | 167 |
| 22: Tim – Sandstone, March, 2013 | 175 |
| 23: Libby – Birmingham, September, 2018 | 186 |
| 24: Josh – The Highlands, September, 2018 | 189 |
| 25: Libby – Birmingham, September, 2018 | 201 |
| **Epilogue** | **213** |
| **Author's Notes** | **221** |

# Prologue

*Libby, Birmingham – July 2019*

Chinks of early morning light pierce my eyes as I strain to open them, and shards of metal penetrate my skull. The pain is unbearable. I wasn't sure how much longer I could bear this torture: I was in urgent need of a Saline Drip and IV Morphine but right now I would settle for a tall glass of water and a couple of paracetamols.

At this very moment however, I was incapable of motion. Every minute movement was an assault on my brain. I was laying comatose in bed, stuck in a post-alcohol afterlife with demon pixies who were concurrently stomping on my grey matter and singing Shania Twain songs with unremitting zeal.

I heard sounds of movement coming from downstairs reminding me that my son Josh and his fiancé, had a couple of houseguests staying. We had all gone out last night celebrating Josh's engagement to Lee and I had suggested that everyone stay over rather than take the last train home which would have ended the evening too early.

My other half had sloped off early in the evening because he had an early shift this morning. His parting words the previous night were along the lines of: "I'm sure you can party for the both of us." I was pretty sure I lived up to that challenge as the pain in my head reasserted itself to remind me exactly how much alcohol I had put away last night.

I whimpered in self-pity and put my head in my hands. I felt dreadful. I gingerly rolled over and picked up my iPhone from the nightstand thinking that I could text Josh – if he would bring me water and paracetamol then I might just survive this whole ghastly episode. I looked at my phone to unlock it using facial recognition:

*Face Not Recognised*
*Try Face ID Again*

*"Oh, for God's sake! Bloody stupid technology,"* I muttered angrily – the effort to hold the phone up to my face becoming too much to bear. I close my eyes, rest for a moment, try to shut out the inconsiderate pixies in my brain singing *"Man I feel Like a Woman"* and attempt facial recognition again*:*

*Face Not Recognised*
*Try Face ID Again*

***"SERIOUSLY?!"***

I feel outraged. I try to ignore the shards of metal penetrating my skull as best as I can and clamber out of bed heading for the en-suite bathroom. I am simultaneously ranting about the ineptitude of technology *'when you really need something to work'* and wincing at the pain in my feet from dancing all night in ridiculously high heels (heels that should be uniquely reserved for restaurant-wear when one merely elegantly walks from the door to the table and remains seated for the duration of the event – with the exception of a visit to the ladies where necessary).

The piercing pain my head was returning and competing with the throbbing of my bunions. Feeling extremely sorry for myself, I glance in the mirror and recoil in horror…

*Oh My God What Has Happened To My Face???*

I am barely recognisable – my nose has doubled in size, it's an enormous bulbous misshapen tomato with an equally sizeable pimple on the end. I say pimple but that does not do it justice – there is a volcanic-like head of pus inside this grotesque knoll ready to erupt at any moment with the ferocity of Mount Vesuvius.

My eyes are puffed, encrusted slits, my hair looks like I've grown the horns of the devil overnight and I have copious amounts of dried drool leading from my mouth to my right ear.

My brain is trying to register a response but: "Face not recognised: Try another mirror" is not having any effect on the situation whatsoever.

And all the while those blasted pixies are singing in my head: "*Man, I feel like a Woman.*"

Let me tell you right now, demon pixies, I do not feel like a woman in any shape or form, I feel like a 300-million-year-old, deep-sea, Slimy Hagfish.

I didn't used to be this person. Where was the happy, sweet youngster I used to be?

# Part 1

# 1
# Libby – Edinburgh, 1983

Moving to Edinburgh from the small town of Cupar, Fife at the age of 18 was daunting and exciting in equal measure. My new job at the Bank of Scotland as a copy typist was going to be the start of a high-flying financial career in the city.

For now, making the tea for Mr Dougald Galbraith, the mortgage section manager, was the only break I had from the temperamental Olivetti typewriter that I was chained to on a daily basis. It wasn't even an electric typewriter – these elite machines were reserved for the more senior typists – or possibly anyone who managed to stay employed at the bank for longer than six months.

I had made a couple of friends at the bank – in particular Ailsa who was my age and was a scream. She was reasonably sensible at work but her fashion sense as soon as she stepped out of the door was something to behold.

Her hair was coloured jet black and, out of work hours it was combed upwards into a gravity-defying style that resembled the bow of a ship, and flat enough on top to play a game of miniature shuffleboard.

Ailsa typically purchased her clothes from charity shops and favoured a Punk/Bohemian fusion that was a style uniquely hers. She was fastidious with her makeup, sporting a very pale complexion and exceptionally chiselled cheekbones. Without exception, she would complete her look with bright red lipstick. With her already tall stature, she was an imposing young woman in anybody's eyes, but I was in awe of her!

I paled into insignificance when I stood next to Ailsa. My wardrobe was a hangover from the recent Lady Di School of Fashion with high frilly collars and (when I was feeling particularly daring) the occasional Pill Box or similar Lady Di-esque styled hat – typically purchased from C & A's.

The wearing of said hats however ended abruptly one evening when Ailsa and I were standing at a bus stop on the corner of Bank Street and Lawnmarket. We were in silhouette against the streetlights when a couple of comedians came out of Deacon Brodies Tavern and jeered at us: *"Jesus ah've seen it a' noo – it's Grace Jones wi' th' Salvation Airmie!"*

To make matters worse, two Medical Students also happened to be waiting at the bus stop (I assumed they were Medical Students since they were carrying an entire library of books between them and were transfixed on Tortora's Anatomy and Physiology as they stood waiting for their bus). On hearing the comedians' comment however, they interrupted their reading and turned their attention to our outfits, making no attempt to hide their amusement. I mean to be fair it *was* very funny, but I decided there and then that I *seriously* needed to have a wardrobe makeover.

Needless to say, Ailsa was not in the slightest bit embarrassed, and having inspected the taller of the students (who happened to be a dead ringer for Clark Kent, complete with dimple and kiss-curl) immediately gave him the benefit of her bountiful charm. I, on the other hand, did my best to imitate a wallflower and disappear into the background until mercifully our bus came along and I managed to pull her away from the delectable Clark Kent much to her disappointment.

❖❖❖

Away from work I lived in a flat in Tollcross. I had a good-sized bedroom and use of the kitchen and bathroom. My bedroom was furnished with a single bed, built-in wardrobe, bookshelf, a small desk and chair, an armchair and a two-seater sofa. There was a fireplace that had been boarded up and no longer in use because storage heaters had been installed to heat the house instead. The carpet in my bedroom was a deep-red, gaudy, highly patterned old-fashioned type similar to something my granny had chosen two decades ago, which absolutely did not match the equally highly patterned, beige wall paper.

There was a dark stain on the wallpaper in one corner above my bed caused an old damp patch that had been repaired well enough not to cause further damage but with no consideration for the aesthetics or decor of the room, so the dark stain remained. I had made an attempt to cover it with a poster, but this just looked odd sitting right in the top corner of the wall. Eventually, one rainy weekend in a rare and for me, outstanding moment of creativity, I draped some floaty fabric over a hoop and hooked that to the ceiling to make a bed canopy that hung directly in front of the stain so it couldn't be seen.

Then feeling rather pleased with my creativity, I cut out some pictures from a magazine of some beautiful, romantic, dreamy-looking girls with porcelain-like skin that looked vaguely medieval in their style. They were from a magazine advertising Anais Anais, my favourite perfume (also frequently and copiously sprayed around my room to rid the room of any whiff of damp).

The pictures looked pretty in the frames I bought from the Grassmarket where I also found an old lace throw for the end of my bed. I even found an old-fashioned wicker shopping basket and filled it with dried flowers to fill the space in front of the boarded-up fireplace. In some lights, the orange and red blooms of the flowers and spikes of the grasses gave the illusion of flames in the fireplace, that I was rather pleased with. The whole effect made the room look much more feminine and romantic.

Of course, it was just for my benefit, nobody else got to see it unfortunately. My Landlady (Phylis) was very strict about having men stay over and my contract actually stated that I was permitted to have guests in my room until 10 pm, after which they must leave the premises. It turned out that she just did not want men staying in her flat full stop since she had her girlfriend staying over on a regular basis.

The contract did seem a little draconian, but the rent was very cheap and my current (and very much foreseeable) single status as far as my love life was concerned did not justify alternative, more costly accommodation.

It surprised me that Phylis was so strict, she was only about ten years older than me. I don't know if she had a bad experience with men previously or was just anti-men because she was gay, but she was very definite with her views.

❖❖❖

My other good friend in Edinburgh was Jenny – an out of work beauty therapist who I met when she was dropping flyers through all the letterboxes in our street. She was offering cheap make-up lessons '*from the comfort of your own home*' so after what I now referred to as *The Salvation Army Incident* and my desire for a wardrobe makeover, I decided this might be a good place to start.

Since it was nearly payday, I had booked an appointment with Jenny the following Saturday afternoon and she turned up with a box-on-wheels full of exotic creams and potions as well as an array of makeup pallets and brushes.

I was pleased with Jenny's reaction to my room when she arrived:

"Oh I love what you have done to your room, it's very pretty, and I like the pre-Raphaelite style you've gone for."

I had absolutely no idea what a pre-Raphaelite style was, she was obviously much more educated than I was and made a mental note to look this up the next time I was near a library.

In addition to her make-up artistry, Jenny obviously extolled the virtues of a cleansing, toning and moisturising routine morning and evening – Pears soap and a flannel would definitely not do, so I was advised to consider purchasing a suitable cleanser, toner and moisturiser and follow a prescribed routine.

It turned out to be a fun afternoon and we ended up spending far more than the allotted time, but Jenny didn't seem to mind. She had worked her magic and the end result was amazing.

"It's a shame I'm not going anywhere now," I said a little forlornly "I'm only going to have to wash this off after all your hard work."

"Well, I'm not doing anything so why don't we go out for a quick drink?" she replied packing all her paraphernalia away.

"Well, if you're sure, there are plenty of bars in this area that we could go to – the Illicit Still isn't far, we could pop in there for a drink?"

And that was the start of our friendship. We found that that we had lots to talk about. It was good to make a friend from outside of work – as much as I enjoyed Ailsa's company, we did tend to end up talking about the bank and the people who worked there. With Jenny, I felt like a completely different person.

Jenny was a year older than me, six inches taller than me and a hundred times more elegant than me. She had long wavy auburn hair and a sense of style straight from Vogue. She had gone to a private girl's school in St Andrews – I used to see the girls from her school with their lacrosse sticks (from a distance) when we played inter-school hockey matches on the pitches by the Old Course Hotel in St Andrews.

Jenny felt that she was not cut out for university but wanted to go into fashion and beauty instead, so her parents indulged her and funded a private beauty course along with a small rented flat in Edinburgh. She had recently qualified as a beauty therapist when I met her.

We both enjoyed music, but Jenny was a mad David Bowie fan and had an enormous life-sized poster of him in her flat. He did look very handsome in the poster – not Clark Kent handsome, but handsome in a camp sort of way.

I was quite surprised that she was such a Bowie fan because I associated his music with an older audience. However, her influence rubbed off on me as she introduced me to his back catalogue. When his new album *Let's Dance* was released, I had already considered myself a fan and when tour dates were announced for the Serious Moonlight Tour and Bowie was to play at Murrayfield on 28th June, Jenny was beside herself. We had to queue all night for tickets.

❖❖❖

The 28th of June couldn't come soon enough and typically it turned out to be a grey, miserable day. My wardrobe for the day remained on the conservative side and comprised of a red, (just slightly) above the knee skirt; a lemon, red and pale blue finely striped t-shirt; a new lemon lambswool V-neck jumper and flat red shoes.

Jenny and I had planned to catch a bus from Princes Street to Murrayfield, but when we got to the bus stop, there were crowds of people who had the same idea and we had no chance of getting on the bus, so we walked to the next stop, and found the same thing so tried the next stop – same problem. At that point, we thought we may as well walk the entire way – it was really only a couple of miles and in flat shoes it wasn't a problem.

We had reached the crossing point by Haymarket Station when I heard an amused voice behind me: "Grace Jones not with you today then?"

I turned around to see Clark Kent – or rather his lookalike – complete with cute dimple but this time with slicked back hair and no kiss curl.

Feeling a flush beginning from my neck travelling up to my cheeks at the memory of our last encounter, I tried to hide my embarrassment with humour.

"I thought you medical students would be too busy cutting up bodies to be concerned about the whereabouts of the delectable Ailsa. What's wrong – have you run out of cadavers to dissect and feeling a bit bored? You need to check out Burke & Hare – I hear they do a marvellous *Grave Robbing and Delivery Service*."

Clark Kent's lookalike had his sidekick with him (I was beginning to think they must be inseparable) who also heard the exchanges, he roared with laughter, slapped him on his back and scoffed:

"Looks like prince charming has lost his charm."

Then turning to me said cheekily.

"Sorry miss – we only let young *Charles* here out on the last Tuesday of every month. I'll take it from here."

The laughter continued at *Young Charles'* expense who gave a shrug of his shoulders then a lingering backward glance from his sidekick as they veered away and headed off towards Haymarket Station.

"That was a bit harsh!" This was Jenny, who until then had been quietly watching the whole episode from a short distance.

I looked at her blankly. "What do you mean? Do you think I was harsh?"

Jenny rolled her eyes and smiled at her friend. "He looked nice – I just thought you might want to have spoken to him rather than scare him off!" She laughed and hooked arms with Libby.

"He *was* gorgeous," I admitted. "I saw him by the Lawnmarket one night when I was out with Ailsa." And I retold the *Salvation Army Saga*, as we both laughed our way along Haymarket Terrace.

❖ ❖ ❖

We had arrived for the concert early and managed to get very close to the stage.

"Whatever we do, we are not moving from here!" Jenny said. "We didn't queue up all night for tickets just to get pushed to the back of the stadium! She was so excited, I, on the other hand, felt like a complete impostor. I really wasn't sure that this was my thing at all and looking around at everyone else. I really didn't feel that I belonged here at all either."

The support bands were OK – although I wasn't very familiar with Ice House, and only recognised *Hey Little Girl* from their Setlist. I had heard of The Thompson Twins though and knew some of their songs from the radio, so I was able to sing along with the hard-core Thompson Twin fan club that had suddenly surrounded us, to songs like *Love on Your Side* and *We are Detectives.*

The rain that had been threatening all day had arrived by the time The Thompson Twins came on, and we were getting very wet. It felt like hours before we actually got to see Bowie and then finally he appeared in his light-coloured suit and what looked like a school tie. He looked incredible. I have to admit, it wasn't until after the first couple of songs had played that I actually recognised anything, but then *'Heroes'* came on and I felt more comfortable and less out of place. I looked at Jenny and she was mesmerised. She couldn't take her eyes from Bowie, she of course was singing along to all the songs, arms waving in the air. She looked exceptionally beautiful with her long red hair, glistening in the rain, she really did look like she could be in a pre-Raphaelite painting.

25

The rain was still lashing down and we were soaking wet, but the closely packed audience made it so hot that steam was actually rising from the crowd. It was more like being in a sauna than a rainstorm.

The concert came to an end with an electrifying encore concluding with *Modern Love*. The atmosphere was incredible: despite my earlier apprehension, I felt elated; like I was dancing on air – and this was not just due to the fact that I was being carried out of the ground by the wave of people exiting en masse.

Everyone left the Stadium with *Modern Love* singing on their lips. There was an outpouring of joy in the air and a sense of camaraderie with everyone heading out of Murrayfield and walking back towards the City Centre. Jenny was glowing, her long hair hung in damp ringlets and her eyes were sparkling.

"That was absolutely amazing Libby! He was absolutely amazing!"

I was about to agree with her when I was jolted from behind and heard some drunken, slurred singing. There was some laughter and a man pointing at my feet then I made out the words *"red dancing shoes"*.

I looked at my feet and at my rather wet, red shoes – that were *so obviously not* made for dancing – then looked up at the face of the person pointing at my shoes. Dimpled chin, kiss curl hanging down with droplets of rain. *God, is this man out to embarrass me for the rest of my life?*

I attempted to smile, feeling very unconfident and unsure as to how I should respond but the ever-present sidekick, fortunately came to my rescue. "Sorry about Charles, he has had seriously too much to drink and he's trying to sing the words to *Let's Dance*. I think your red shoes must have set him off!"

Charles looked at me with big sad eyes, his bottom lip in a comedy droop:

"Aaaw don't you wanna dance with me?"

He looked mildly confused for a second, then smiled, slurred his way tunelessly through more lyrics, butchering every line. Then he abruptly stopped singing and tried to focus on something that appeared to be on my jumper. He closed one eye, turned his head slightly as if this might help him focus, then said very slowly, trying to enunciate each word so that it came out correctly but comprehensively failed to achieve this:

"What…has…happent…to…hyuuuur…jummmpha?"

"I'm sorry? What has happened to what?" I replied.

"Hyuuuur jummmpha!" he said pointing towards my midriff.

An entourage of males had surrounded him by this time, including his trusted sidekick who started pulling him away. "Come on, Charlie Boy, leave this young lady alone!"

Turning to me, his friend apologised for the third time that day: "Sorry Miss…er…?"

"Libby – I'm Libby…and this is Jenny," I said, trying to bring my friend into the conversation so that I was not the sole centre of attention but then it suddenly dawned on me what *Charlie Boy* was trying to say. I looked down at my new lemon coloured, lambswool jumper and incredibly, it had shrunk! With the pouring rain and the heat from the concert, it was like my jumper had gone through a tumble dryer and dried onto me two or three sizes smaller. The cuffs were now closer to my elbows than my wrists and the bottom of the jumper did not come near to meeting the waistband of my skirt.

*"What has happened to my jumper?"* I cried.
*"What…has…happent…to…hyuuuur…jummmpha?"* Charles slurred.
*"What has happened to your jumper?"* Jenny laughed.

Everyone in the little group were now looking at me or rather looking at my shrunken jumper that would now be better suited to a ten-year-old. Charles was the first to state the obvious: "I… think… hyuur… jummpha… is… shrunnnnkkk."

He looked so genuinely crestfallen at the state of my jumper that I burst out laughing, much to the relief of everyone else who didn't seem like they were able to hold in their laughter for much longer anyway.

"Well Libby," said Charles's sidekick "I'm Tim by the way and this fellow, as you know, is Charles and usually, we would be the first to step in and solve The Mystery of The Incredible Shrinking Jumper. But unfortunately, as much as we'd love to stay and solve this mystery, we will have to run I'm afraid because I need to get this lot back to Haymarket Station then get him (nodding his head towards Charles) back to the flat. Sorry to dash off like this but hopefully we'll bump into you both again. Bye for now ladies."

"Bye fur noww ladiesssss," slurred Charles. "Gifff my luvv to Grace Jones," he giggled and nearly fell over at his own hysterics.

We could hear the group singing as they carried on down the road towards the city centre and could just about make out the words despite Charles's slurring.

❖ ❖ ❖

The following weekend, we were in Jenny's flat laughing about the mystery of the incredible shrinking jumper and talking about Charles and Tim.

"That's the kind of situation I could only dream about you know. I'd love to meet someone gorgeous and then they bump into you out of the blue and ask you out."

"You know," said Jenny, "I think Charles really wanted to talk to you back there."

"No, he wasn't, he was asking about Ailsa – he asked where she was. I'm just too awkward for anyone like him to be interested in me."

"Don't you dare put yourself down," said Jenny sharply.

I was in no doubt about my analysis of the situation, and I sat in Jenny's flat feeling rather forlorn because not only had I squandered any possible future association between myself and the lovely Charles, now Jenny was cross with me because I disclosed my own self-doubt. I gave a long sigh.

"I actually think Tim was rather dishy," Jenny said, breaking the glum mood that had suddenly descended.

"Really?" I was amazed! "I thought you had eyes for nobody but Hugo?!"

Hugo was the son of very wealthy family friend of her father. The enigmatic Hugo travelled all around Europe and had a vague romantic attachment to Jenny. He would turn up at the drop of a hat bringing her beautiful gifts; wine and dine her extravagantly for several days (and nights), and then disappear again for weeks at a time. Because of this attachment, she kept herself unobtainable in terms of any other relationships.

"You know I have eyes for nobody but Hugo," Jenny smiled inwardly to herself. "I just thought that Tim looked rather dishy – a nice man – that's all!"

"Mmmm. I know what you mean about Tim, he's more sort of *dashing* and *dependable*, unlike Charles who is more *gorgeous* but *irresponsible.*"

"Yes, that's exactly what I mean, I wouldn't trust Charles with your heart at all!"

❖❖❖

# 2
# Tim – Edinburgh, 1983

I spotted her as soon as they arrived at the bus stop. We'd just finished a late lecture on renal physiology and were still pondering over what might affect the glomerular filtration rate for our tutorial the following morning.

Her friend was larger than life, but it was the quiet one who caught my eye. Some joker came out of the pub and made a comment about the way they were dressed – mainly down to the louder one's quirky sense of style. I could see that the quiet one was mortified, but I could also see the humour in her eyes, I think she found it quite funny. Those all-seeing eyes – I'm sure she could see everything with those eyes. She took everything in; observing everything and everybody – she'd make a good Doctor!

Of course, Charles had to smirk at them and start laughing – he can be such a prat! That's him all over, then he turns on the charm and all the girls just fall over themselves. He's been the same since I met him in in first year. Interestingly it was only the quirky one who was responding to Charles this time. But I found the quiet one with the big eyes intriguing.

I didn't get to speak to her though because their bus came along, and she disappeared into the Edinburgh night.

Charles was still smirking when they left.

"Grace Jones and the Salvation Army! Hilarious! She was quite something though. Although I think she might very well eat you for breakfast – a bit racy for you Tim?"

"Quite probably," I said but thinking instead about the quiet girl with the large, knowing, all-seeing eyes and wondering if I would ever see her again.

❖ ❖ ❖

We'd had a long academic term of practical's, research, exams, and clinical skills. The exams, including all the clinical exams were over and the summer break was finally here. We had kept our flat in New Town for the summer as we both intended to find summer jobs and we were renting the same flat in the next academic year. But for the next few weeks we had prescribed ourselves lots of sleep!

At the end of June, Bowie was playing at Murrayfield. We managed to get hold of some tickets and had arranged to meet up with some friends from Glasgow on the day of the concert and travel to Murrayfield together.

We had nearly reached Haymarket Station to meet our friends when I saw in front of us the girl with the lovely eyes. She was with a different friend this time, though there was something vaguely familiar about her friend – she was a very beautiful girl, but aloof with a definite air of 'unobtainable' emanating from her. I said, turning to Charles: "Isn't that the girl we saw at the bus stop?"

We had stopped at the crossing point at that moment. The two girls were in front of us and had turned to watch for traffic – it was definitely the girl from the bus stop. In a loud brash voice, Charles shouted to her: "Grace Jones not with you today then?"

She turned around and I saw that she immediately recognised him. There was also that look that I always see when women look at Charles – desire, I think, you would call it. I saw her colour a little, but she was feisty and snapped back a response – something amusing about dissecting cadavers, and about the grave robbers, Burke & Hare so she must have already clocked that we were medical students.

She had a despondent look about her too, a sadness that made me feel protective of her. I steered Charles away to stop him making any further rude remarks, making a joke of him losing his touch, but I couldn't resist taking a look back at her as we walked towards Haymarket Station, wondering how I could see her again but without Charles getting in the way. There was just something so lovely about her.

We met up with the Glasgow crew and decided to go for a quick pint as there was plenty of time before the start of the concert. Two and a half hours later, having graced several local hostelries at Charles's insistence – Charles having sampled a number of alcoholic beverages and chatted up as many girls as he possibly could – we managed to get into the stadium just before the start of Bowie's set. We had missed the support bands and it was pouring down with rain but we got to see Bowie live.

Charles was still rather drunk at the end of the concert, but the atmosphere was electric. Everyone was singing Bowie songs and walking back to the City Centre together. Suddenly Charles had pushed through a throng of people and was dancing around someone, pointing at their feet. I couldn't believe it, but it was the same girl – again!

He was trying to sing something but slurring and mixing up the words. Charles was making a fool of himself; the girl was once more holding her own. She was either completely disinterested in him or playing it very cool.

Then the very drunk Charles for some inexplicable reason started to make fun of her jumper so at that point I decided to intervene. I managed to introduce myself and find out her name then made some lame apologies saying that the Glasgow boys needed to get their train back and that I needed to get Charles back to the flat.

Back at the flat, Charles had crashed onto the sofa and fell asleep. I left him there with a pillow behind his head, and covered him with a blanket, then left a pint of water and some paracetamol on the table next to him. He probably wouldn't thank me for it but I couldn't see anyone suffer unnecessarily, not even Charles! Why did I put up with him?

I can't stop thinking about this girl. I've bumped into her three times now and always with Charles. Twice I've had to make a quick exit because he was being an idiot. I wonder if I could ever meet her again – without Charles getting in the way.

❖ ❖ ❖

The start of the new academic year was fast approaching. I couldn't believe we had already completed two years! My summer bar job had allowed me to save some money to help with living costs for the next year and my grandpa had sent me a generous cheque for my birthday as he always did. It makes me smile to think of him.

We've always been close: I remember when I went off to Prep School, he would send an extra Tuck Box telling me not to mention it to Grandma. I make a mental note to remind myself to write and thank him and let him know how I am. It saddens me to think of him living alone since Grandma died. It's been over ten years now, but he says he's content to live out his days in the house that they shared together with all their memories. He's an old romantic really; I can see what Grandma would have loved about him. The pictures of him as a young man showed him as a confident, debonair and chivalrous gentleman, but he was more than that, there is a strength and an unwavering reliability about him. If I could be half the man he is, I would be a very happy man.

I put the cheque in my wallet for safekeeping thinking I could bank it on the way to library later that day, then decide to go for a walk as the sun was shining for a change.

My walk took me down Hanover Street with the intention of going along Princes Street into the Gardens, but then I thought I may as well take a slight detour to the bank and deposit my cheque, so I carried on past Waverley Station and up The Mound to the Bank of Scotland.

I didn't have my deposit book with me, so I needed to fill in a deposit slip. The box where the slips should have been kept was empty so rather than queue twice, I gesticulated towards the cashier that the box was empty and they sent a junior to fill the box.

As the girl came closer, I thought I recognised her. She looked very much like Libby's friend from the bus stop, but without the flamboyant hair and quirky dress sense she was hard to recognise, but I was pretty sure it was her. *I really should say something to her – this could be the only way I could ever orchestrate another meeting with Libby.*

"Excuse me miss, but I think we've met before."

Standing appraising me with one hand on her hip, she thought for a minute. There appeared to be absolutely no sign of recognition whatsoever, in fact she was now looking at me like I had two heads. I felt like I was in danger of her pressing a secret emergency button or possibly an ejector button that would shoot me through the domed roof of the 18$^{th}$ century building or spraying me with some deadly chemical aerosol that would blind me for eternity.

I noticed that she had a name badge on advising customers of her name 'Ailsa' and remembered Libby saying something to Charles about the *delectable Ailsa.* At the moment, she was looking more like fearsome Ailsa – she was, as Charles rightly pointed out, quite capable of eating me for breakfast.

Eventually she replied "That's th' warst chat up line ah've ever heard – if ye want tae ask me out, yoo'll hae tae dae better than 'at!"

Oh God, this really wasn't going well at all. "No, no, sorry, I stammered, I think my friend and I met you at a bus stop on Bank Street, by the Lawnmarket, a few months ago. Someone told you that you looked like Grace Jones."

"Grace Jones?" She snorted, "Have ye seen mah peely-wally skin? Diz...this look..." She stopped suddenly in mid-sentence, then continued less abrasively, dropping the broad Scots brogue "Grace Jones and the Salvation Army?" She finished with a grin on her face. That was you?

"Yes...No, that wasn't me, but my friend and I were at the bus stop and he, my friend I mean, was chatting with you and then you and Libby got your bus?"

"He was chatting with me at the bus stop?" She said looking slightly more interested in the conversation.

"Err, yes."

"Good looking bloke, looks like Clark Kent, dimple on his chin and a kiss curl?" she asked.

I sighed deeply. *God, how do they remember things like that?* "Yes, that's Charles," I acknowledged.

"How do you know Libby?" she asked obviously now very curious that I would know her name.

"I don't really know her, but I bumped into her again at Murrayfield after the Bowie Concert. I only know her name. Look I know this sounds a bit feeble, but could you tell her that I was asking for her? I'm Tim. Tim from the Bowie Concert. But not the drunk one, that was Charles. I was the sensible one. The non-drunk one. I'd really like to speak to her again. Meet her again. Buy her a coffee. A drink?"

I was sounding desperate; it was all going a bit pear-shaped. I should just leave now while I was still standing on two feet and not pleading on bended knees or worse still grovelling and snivelling and making an absolute arse of myself.

I looked at Ailsa, she was scribbling something on a piece of paper.

"I'm not going to give you Libby's number, but I will talk to her and you can give me your number. If she wants it, I'll give it to her. This is my number," she said giving me the note she had written. "You might want to share this with your friend – Charles, was it? It may help me remember to speak to Libby if he happens to call me for another chat."

I gave her my number and took hers, thanking her for her time and help, and turned to walk away but she stopped me.

"Haven't you forgotten something?"

I stopped and looked around, puzzled, then she gave me a blank deposit slip.

"Can I help you with your deposit slip sir," she said, her professionalism suddenly returning as a more senior person appeared behind her.

"Err…no…thank you Miss…err…Ailsa." I said looking at her name badge again. You have been most helpful.

"There's a cashier free over there if you want to go straight ahead," she said brusquely then walked back towards the studded, padded security doors to her desk.

I deposited my cheque in a daze, hoping that Ailsa would talk to Libby. I had Ailsa's number so could phone if I hadn't heard anything in a few days. The question was, should I pass this on to Charles or not, knowing his past history with women?

# 3
# Libby – Edinburgh, 1983

Jenny has invited me to a charity cricket match this coming weekend. I mean, Cricket? I know absolutely nothing about cricket! Do people actually play cricket in Scotland? I'm not overenthusiastic about it, but Jenny is really excited and really wants me to come with her, and she can be very persuasive!

Apparently, the family of one of her old school friends have arranged the charity match in the grounds of their home. It must be a big garden – I can't imagine my mum and dad agreeing to have a cricket match of any sort in our back garden! I'm guessing it must be a scaled-down version, like they do with five-a-side football maybe? Who knows?

She told me that her friends' family home is not far from Edinburgh – about 20 miles away, near Haddington. She thinks it's going to be fun and that I'd really enjoy myself so she's coming round to my flat tonight to help me decide what to wear.

The weather for the weekend is forecast to be warm and sunny for a change so Jenny suggested wearing a dress and has even brought a few items that I might want to try on. Unfortunately, whilst Jenny looked like she had just stepped off the front cover of a Laura Ashley brochure in her lovely dresses, everything that Jenny brought for me to try on made me look like I had just stepped out of Little House on the Prairie. Apart from the fact that everything was far too long for me, it all made me look rather frumpy. In the end we settled on a loose, short-sleeved blouse with a flattering slashed neckline and a long floaty skirt, nipped in at the waist with a wide belt. I was also considering a wide brimmed straw hat, but would make that decision on the day depending on the weather. I was still smarting a little from the Salvation Army incident so hat-wearing was still a traumatic experience for me!

❖ ❖ ❖

The day of the charity cricket match did indeed turn out to be a rare, glorious sunny August day. Jenny drove us there in a borrowed car. She said it was just south of Haddington so when I saw signs for Haddington, I started looking out for a large house that might be suitable for such an event. What I wasn't expecting to see was an enormous historic, A-Listed house, *Chranachlove House*, with a 15$^{th}$ Century tower and a coach House set in wooded estates and acres of land. When we arrived, the grounds were even more impressive. There were a series of marquees erected at one of the lower fields, below the manicured lawns, about ten minutes stroll from the main house, close to a set of converted stables. I was informed that the three marquees were to provide a bar; to serve the cricket tea, and to act as a pavilion for the cricket players. Close to the marquees, a cricket pitch was marked out with a boundary rope, a *cricket strip* and *wickets* (thankfully I managed not to make a joke about these final pieces of information because I later learned that one was the strip of grass where the batsmen ran up and down to score runs, and the other was the wooden stumps that were knocked down to get the batsmen out!)

Set back from the boundary rope were numerous deck chairs for the spectators. This was no back garden game of cricket – it was clearly very professionally thought out and I found everything rather overwhelming – especially when Jenny introduced me to the family of her school friend: the Earl and Countess of Chranachlove House.

The Earl explained that the Chranachlove Shield Charity Match took place every year and that he selected his own team (The Earl's XI) to play against the local cricket club. The Earl's XI invariably came from the sons of family friends who played cricket for their school or university teams. He explained that local side had won for the last five years but that he had high hopes for his team this year. As the match was due to start, I was encouraged to make myself at home and help myself to refreshments, with the additional advice that the fruit punch came with a health warning, being extremely potent and alcoholic but that the iced tea was very refreshing. I was also advised to be seated when play was in progress as the cricketers took this game very seriously and would not be impressed with anyone wandering around during play.

It was getting very warm, and I was glad that I opted for the sun hat in the end, but decided to find some shade too. Jenny had already excused herself, so I quickly helped myself to some iced tea and walked over to the boundary to some deck chairs in a shaded spot to watch the game.

I found myself sitting next to an elderly gentleman who nodded politely to me as I sat down. As instructed, I sat quietly and took in the events of the game – a game of which I had absolutely no understanding whatsoever.

The gentleman next to me appeared to be making a series of dots and dashes and adding a few numbers into a book lined with different sized boxes on the page. I looked intently at the game as it was being played and tried to fathom how this correlated with the dots, dashes and numbers being entered into the book by the elderly gentleman next to me. I was so intent on trying to unravel this strange algorithm – by watching the game, then looking to see what he would mark on his paper – that I didn't notice that he was watching me.

"Do you score?" he asked.

"I'm sorry?" I asked astonished at such a question.

"It's just that you look like you are checking my scoring, so I wondered if you were a scorer," he clarified.

"Oh goodness, no – I'm so sorry," I said feeling my cheeks flush, "I have never even been to a cricket match before in my life. I was just trying to figure out what all the dashes and dots meant in your book. I'm so sorry, I didn't mean to intrude, or interrupt you. I'm really sorry."

I was babbling again – it always happened when I was embarrassed; I presented with verbal diarrhoea and couldn't stop words coming out of my mouth.

The gentleman smiled kindly and said "I only do this because it helps me to follow the game, and at my age, it keeps my mind active."

I smiled back, "I was thinking it looks very complicated. There seems like a lot to follow."

"It looks more difficult than it actually is," he said, "the next over is about to start so I'll talk you through it if you like."

Before long, I had found out that an *over* meant that a bowler had bowled six balls to a batsman; I learned that the dots and dashes in the boxes were records of all the balls that the bowlers had bowled. I found out that each batsman also had a running score and where these dots and numbers should be entered. There was also another entry where you could see a tally of the total score throughout the game and a record of 'extras' (such as where a ball was bowled too wide for the batsman to reach). It really was very complicated.

My new tutor (who I found out was called Philip) was very patient with me and explained everything in a way that was genuinely interesting. The game stopped being tedious and boring but became a fast-paced, exciting sport with so much to concentrate on. I also found out that there were ten different ways to get a batsman out, but I hadn't quite got to grips with that yet.

After a while, there was a lull in the game with only dots being placed against the batsman's names and dots in the bowler's boxes. I wondered if Philip was getting a bit bored as he had started to join up the dots at this stage, to form a capital 'M' in the boxes. But I was gently informed with only slight rolling of Phillip's eyes that this meant a maiden over had been bowled, meaning that no runs had been scored from that over and that if the dots had been joined up to form a 'W', this would mean that it was a wicket maiden – that the bowler would have taken a wicket (got someone out) and also scored no runs in that over. There really was so much to take in.

The lull continued, then all of a sudden, several things happened at once. Firstly, there was a loud crack and the stumps seemed to split apart, several players jumped up and down and started shouting at the umpire, holding their index fingers at him. Phillip who until then had presented with a quiet, calm and gentile demeanour, suddenly shouted "Bowled him! What a googly."

I was startled and jumped so much at this remarkable outburst that I nearly dropped my glass and my deckchair almost collapsed underneath me.

I looked at the players, who were surrounding another tall player, slapping him on the back and shoulders and tousling his hair and generally congratulating him with shouts of, "Well bowled Tiddler," and "Got him Tiddler!"

I looked quizzically at Phillip who was writing on his score sheet, smiling and said, "He has a lovely googly."

"Really?" I said, "And you can see that from all the way over here?" Still bemused I looked intently at the tall player again, frowning and wondering what he could see that I couldn't. Phillip chortled and now back to his calm and gentle manner explained that a googly was a way of delivering a ball.

He explained that the bowler had flicked his wrist so that it changed the direction that the ball was spinning. The batsman had thought it would go in the other direction, but instead it flew right between his bat and his pads and hit the wicket and he was bowled out – one of the ten ways in which a batsman could be out – only another nine to learn!

The batsman was walking back to the makeshift pavilion carrying out some imaginary practice shots with his bat as if he was trying to replay the shot that got him out. As he made his way towards the marquee, everybody clapped but he looked very cross with himself and stomped his way past the spectators. "That was their best batsman," Phillip told me. "He prides himself on spotting a googly, but he must have lost concentration for a second. So, I make that 130 for one," he said completing the batsman's total in the correct box. "That's just a quick way of saying they have 130 runs for one wicket," he continued with a smile.

I looked back at the game, there were a few position changes with the fielders then the bowler had taken up his position again and a new batsman was standing at the stumps – or the crease as Phillip had corrected, but after all the excitement of the last ball, the over ended with a dot ball.

"Dot ball to end the over then. That's my grandson out there," said Phillip, "He does have a lovely bowling action, a slow bowler with a nice, high action and able to disguise the delivery of the ball from the hand so it's difficult for the batsman to see the seam and pick out the spin."

"Oh? I hadn't realised that your grandson was playing. Is that the one they're calling Tiddler?" Phillip's face clouded over, and I could see that there was something in his thoughts that made him uneasy. I waited quietly, not wanting to intrude on his thoughts but not knowing how to change the subject.

The umpire signalled for a drinks break and broke the tension a little. Some of the batting team ran on to the pitch with jugs of orange squash and plastic tumblers to give the players a drink.

I looked at Phillip who was gazing thoughtfully, but it was as though he could see things in his mind's eye. When he eventually spoke, his voice was full of sadness: "I think nicknames are a contentious issue. Some people think they are a leveller: what I mean by that is that they allow everyone to be brought down to the same level – for instance, my grandson went to a school where everyone had a nickname. You could be the son of an Earl or the son of a banker but by giving a boy a nickname you wouldn't know anything about them. On the face of it, it sounds like a good idea. The problem is that the people who assign these nicknames are usually the ones who have more power or control in a group, or are higher up the chain, and they usually find some *so-called* flaw in that person's character or something to make a joke out of, to create a nickname. Then that nickname is something that dehumanises and demoralises you, everybody calls you by this new name, it becomes your new identity, and replaces the things that you are familiar with. And these names can live on for years – there's always someone from an old school or somewhere from your past that will remember that name and bring back an old memory or an old fear. I don't know why schools condone this behaviour, it should have been banned years ago."

I felt so sad for this kind and gentle man. I wasn't sure if he was reflecting on his own experience or his grandson's experience. I thought back to how I felt about the *Salvation Army Incident*. I was an adult and yet I had wanted the ground to open up and swallow me when those two jokers at the bus stop referred to Ailsa and myself as Grace Jones and the Salvation Army. It had already impacted on the way I was dressing and choosing clothes. Imagine how I would feel if I was a child, and on a daily basis, people referred to the incident and made a nickname for me because of this one incident. I really could see Phillip's perspective. I took a deep breath and let it out slowly before I replied:

"Gosh, Phillip, that is something that I had really never considered before, but I can understand how traumatic this could be for a child – or an adult, or me if I'm honest. Having a name imposed on you and used to torment you as a child is so cruel. It really is a terrible form of bullying."

Phillip looked at me with his pale blue, slightly watery eyes and smiled his kindly smile, nodding his head. "Yes, I believe you do understand," he said, "I can see that you have a good soul and a kind heart. My grandson had quite a time of it, but that's his story to tell if you ever meet him."

"I'm not sure about having a good soul and a kind heart," I said blushing, "but maybe one day I will meet your grandson, and if he is as lovely as you, then I would be very happy to meet him! But in the meantime, before the next over starts, can I get you anything to drink at all, I think I need to stretch my legs a little."

"Take your time my dear, but an iced tea would be marvellous – I trust that someone has warned you about the lethal punch?"

"Absolutely – the two main pieces of advice I was given on arrival were: *avoid the punch* and *don't interrupt play*! So with that in mind, I'll be back with your iced tea between overs."

I walked quickly back to the marquee where I found Jenny being lavishly entertained by Hugo. There was an almost empty bottle of champagne in an ice bucket on the table between them and a plate of canapés although the latter had barely been touched.

Jenny waved and called me over to their table, but I hesitated, not wanting to intrude on their cosy drinks corner. Jenny came over to me and took me by the arm.

"Oh, there you are Libby, I wondered where you'd got to. I'm so sorry that I abandoned you. I wasn't sure if Hugo was going to be here today, but he turned up and – well, the time seems to have just disappeared. What have you been up to all this time? I hope you haven't been bored. Do come over and join us."

"Jenny, I'm actually desperate to find a loo," I said before she dragged me over to their table.

"Yes of course, come with me," she said taking charge, "I could do with freshening up myself, it's dreadfully muggy isn't it?" She waved at Hugo and said, "We'll be back in a tick Hugo."

It seemed that time spent with Hugo had given Jenny an extra plum or two in her mouth as her accent had gone all public school. I said nothing but allowed her to steer me away from the table. We were heading towards the old stable block which had been converted into six small flats, but for today it had been commandeered as toilet facilities.

Jenny explained to me that the Earl was intending to rent the flats to his staff, but that he hadn't got round to furnishing them yet, so they decided to make use of all the bathrooms today: four bathrooms were designated as the male toilets (since there were two cricket teams to cater for) and two bathrooms were designated female toilets.

Jenny and I had caught up with each other's news by the time we got back to the marquee. Jenny's big gossip was that Hugo's sister Daisy had dated half of the earl's cricket team but that was possibly an exaggeration and that it may have just been one or two of the players. "Lucky her, either way," I said laughing as we returned to her table. Hugo was also striding back to the table brandishing another bottle of champagne and two extra glasses. I turned to Jenny: "Will you be OK to drive back to Edinburgh?" I asked, feeling alarmed.

Hugo brushed my question aside and informed us that he would arrange transport back to Edinburgh. I wasn't sure what that actually meant, but I guessed that he was wealthy enough to arrange for a 20-mile taxi ride back to the city.

Then Jenny further added to my concern when she whispered to me that she and Hugo were to spend the night at Chranachlove House as the earl's guests and that Hugo would be dashing off somewhere exotic again in the morning so she wouldn't see him for another month. I did wonder why she hadn't told me this in private when we were in the bathroom. I felt very unsure of my situation, and it felt rather unfair of Jenny to put me in this predicament. She must have recognised that I was feeling insecure because she manoeuvred me away from Hugo and in a gentle tone, explained that there were a number of people driving back to Edinburgh later this evening and that any one of them would be happy to give me a lift and that I had nothing to worry about. She assured me that we would all be able to talk to everybody after the match so I wouldn't be getting into a stranger's car. She would make sure that I was comfortable with whomever was giving me a lift.

"Would you like to join us for some champagne," she asked as we again returned to their table. "No, I'd better not, thanks all the same. I have to go to work tomorrow, and champagne gives me a terrible headache. I have been sitting with someone by the boundary and I promised I would bring him back an iced tea – he will be wondering where I am." Jenny's eyebrow raised in a questioning look, and she grinned at me.

"There's nothing to get excited about Jenny," I said, "he is watching his grandson play in the match and he was explaining some of the rules of the game to me!"

"Oh, I see," she said laughing, "well as long as you are OK and having fun."

I considered this for a second, it was quite an exceptional day and something that I had never experienced before. I could have been sitting in my flat on my own but instead I was sitting in a beautiful setting, chatting to a charming elderly man who was teaching me the rudiments of a game that I knew nothing about. The sun was shining, and I was happy. "I am actually," I smiled at Jenny. "Thank you for inviting me, I'm having a lovely time and I'm sorry that I was a bit uptight about getting home. I will be absolutely fine."

"I'm so pleased," Jenny replied, "I was feeling guilty about abandoning you."

I had assured Jenny that I was more than happy to go back and watch the cricket. So I made my excuses to her and Hugo and collected two iced teas, waited for the end of the Over and headed back to my seat next to Phillip.

# 4
# Tim – Edinburgh, 1983

This was my fourth year of playing for the Earl's XI in the 40-over Charity Shield. I remember as a child how desperate I was to be picked – it was considered a badge of honour at our school if one had been picked by the Earl to play for his team. I smiled now thinking of how excited and nervous I was the first time I played. The two new young players picked this year were handy with a bat and were top of the batting averages for their respective schools' First XI, so they could be useful today.

The captain had given a good team talk so we were raring to go; we had won the toss and chosen to bowl. The quick bowlers and medium pacers had done a good job and taken the shine off the new ball nicely but by the 17th over we still hadn't taken any wickets.

The captain had brought me on to bowl at a good time: it was the 18th over and the ball had more grip and control for me to spin it. I just needed to make sure that I could hide the seam and disguise the delivery of the ball. My first over was a bit of a loosener but I managed to keep a clean sheet and bowl a maiden over. My friend James bowled opposite me and again bowled a Maiden, but we just couldn't get a wicket.

It was my turn to bowl again, I was bowling the 20$^{th}$ over: four more dot balls. I needed to do something here, this batsman was tricky. I needed to disguise the spin so just before I released the next ball, I flicked my wrist: the ball came out of my hand with a clockwise spin, and I knew that it would pitch and head straight towards the batsman's legs and away from where he was expecting it to go.

Yes! Got him! We were all ecstatic. Everyone was jumping up and down, calling to the umpire "*How was he?!*" The umpire's finger went up and finally we had our man! I was buzzing, everyone was congratulating me. But then I heard that old nickname from school being shouted out: "Well bowled, Tiddler."

That was Jez, I only vaguely knew him but, what a twat! He wasn't in my house at school but somehow, he knew and never seemed to forget that bloody nickname. God, I hated that name. That one ghastly episode in my life from school that haunted me. I was 20 years old, nearly 21, but just hearing that name brought me crashing straight back to that wretched time in my first year of boarding school. I was finding it difficult to concentrate, but I had to shake this off and get back to the game. I looked around the ground and saw Grandpa in his usual spectator's spot. He was looking my way and nodding so I know that he had heard it and that he was sending me a message of support in his typically understated way.

I had only just pulled myself together in time to clap the batsman off the pitch. I had one more ball to bowl for this over, then it would be the drinks interval. I asked the skipper to move the *long on* fielder to come in five yards – not because I needed him to move, but because it gave me an extra minute to calm down. A few more deep breaths, then to my great relief, I bowled a dot ball.

❖❖❖

The end of the drink's interval brought some cloud cover, so the seam bowlers were brought back on. It was the type of hot and close afternoon that was distracting to the batsmen, and we took a flurry of wickets shortly after drinks. From 130 for 1, we were suddenly 142 for 4, then one of the batsmen called for a run that should never have been taken. The ball had landed to the side of me at backward square leg. I collected the ball and had the wicket in my line of sight, the batsman was still two yards out. I aimed and threw the ball in a single movement. The ball hit the bails – a direct hit, no question, a run out – amazing we were 142 for five!

Again, there was uproar and lots of congratulating. Jez was in my ear again, rubbing my head. "Nice one, Tiddler." But this time I reciprocated – I grabbed his hair roughly, at the base of his neck. He glared at me, but I stared him down. I was a good six inches taller than him and knew that I could, at a push, be mildly intimidating when I was railed: "It's Tim, or Timothy to you, so stop being a moron. You're not a schoolboy anymore, OK?" I gave an extra tug of the hair at the base of his neck to make sure he had got the message; it was a bit school boyish on my part to be fair but I needed to draw a line under this and stop his behaviour.

"All right mate, sorry. No harm meant. Just a bit of banter you know?"

My response was to just shake my head and look at him pitifully, but I think the nod of my head accompanied with narrowed eyes provided the warning look that was required, and he had the decency to look churlish and walk away.

James walked up to me and gave me a compassionate, understanding look. He placed his hand gently on my shoulder in support.

I shrugged and said with a laugh to release the tension "Just someone who needed putting in their place." He nodded and replied: "I think he got the message."

❖❖❖

The middle order batsmen were proving difficult to dislodge and quickly made a partnership of 50 runs. We were now 192 for five but we only had five overs left to bowl them out. The batsmen were picking up runs off every ball at the moment and the run rate was creeping up to eight an over. The overs were ticking by, and time was running out, we were now down to two overs and still hadn't taken any more wickets.

Then finally, one of the batsmen aimed a big heave right back over the bowler's head but hit it straight to James at *long off* who gratefully caught it. They were now 229 for six with only eight more balls left, this could be a good score. It wouldn't be a bad chase if we could keep the last over tight.

There were two more dot balls to finish this over, then we were on to the final over.

They ran two singles in succession off the first two balls, then a dot ball, another dot ball, two more runs scored off the fifth ball, then it was the final ball of the innings. The batsman attempted a sweep, but he caught the edge of his bat and the ball looped into the sky. The skipper steadied himself underneath, ready to catch it – and OUT! The end of the innings and they were 232 for seven. We needed 233 to win. That was definitely doable. But for now, we were heading to the marquee for the tea interval. The cricket tea was usually quite something, so we were looking forward to it.

❖❖❖

I quickly freshened up using the facilities provided and by the time I got back to the marquee, I saw James talking to his ex-girlfriend Daisy. He caught up with me and we joined the queue for tea and sandwiches and possibly some cake if there was any left by the time we got there.

"How are things between you and Daisy?" I asked, "I thought you had cooled things off?"

"Oh, it's definitely off, she has moved on to pastures new and good luck to her to be honest! But her brother Hugo is here with his girlfriend Genevieve and typically he's domineered the whole situation so now Genevieve's friend has been left high and dry without a lift back to Edinburgh. Daisy was hoping that I could take the friend back with me this evening but I'm staying local so that I can have a few drinks."

I vaguely remembered Daisy's brother and his grandiose ways and superior manner; seemingly everyone had to comply with his demands, regardless of who got in his way.

"Oh dear, well if the poor girl is still stuck for a lift, I'm heading back to Edinburgh tonight so I could give her a lift. I'm sure she will be mortified at being offered a lift by a complete stranger though so you will have to vouch for me!"

James laughed and said that he would most definitely put in a good word for me.

The skipper wanted to give another team talk before our second innings, so we all made our way back towards the makeshift pavilion in the other marquee. The batting order was decided, with me batting down the order to allow the two young batsmen to show us what they had. And what an incredible innings we had: as the Earl had predicted, this was actually his year. We got the required runs with ten overs to spare, largely due to the huge partnership of the young batsmen who were hitting 4s and 6s all over the field. Needless to say, I wasn't required to bat, or even to pad up so had an enjoyable afternoon watching some good amateur cricket.

Presentations were over, Man of the Match was awarded, and I hadn't had a chance to speak to Grandpa yet, so I made my excuses and went to find him. By the time I had made my way towards Grandpa's usual spot, he was already being helped to his feet by a young woman. She had her back to me so I couldn't see who it was, but it definitely wasn't anybody I'd seen accompanying Grandpa previously. I know he occasionally needed some additional care and support with his arthritis but this person didn't strike me as having that sort of approach, so I was curious to know who was helping him.

"Did you enjoy the game, Gramps?" I shouted as I drew closer, to gain their attention.

"My dear boy yes, I did, immensely! A superb game. And we were just saying how much we enjoyed your googlies."

"Ha, Gramps, the old ones are the best, eh?"

The young woman giggled as she turned around, our eyes meeting. I took a sharp intake of breath hardly believing what I was seeing.

"Elizabeth," Grandpa was saying, "let me introduce you to my grandson, Timothy. I've talked about him so much today, I'm so pleased that you have had a chance to meet him."

"Hello Tim, we've actually met before, but you might remember me as Libby." The calmness of her voice was betrayed by the flush that started in her neck and worked its way up to her cheeks, but she gave me a big smile and continued, "If I'm being called Elizabeth, it's usually because I've done something wrong so, please call me Libby or I'll think I'm in trouble!"

I laughed, and nodded, wishing I could be a little more debonaire. "Yes, the last time we met we were trying to solve mystery of the incredible shrinking jumper, do you remember?" Libby laughed loudly, "Yes, I do! It got so wet at the concert, then it was so incredibly hot with everybody dancing so closely together, that my jumper literally dried like it was in a tumble dryer." Grandpa looked back and forth between us, bemused.

"Well, what a remarkable coincidence that you two know each other!"

Libby and I looked at each other, our eyes meeting again. "I'm not sure we do know each other really," she said, "but we do seem to keep bumping into each other – it's rather odd really!"

"Libby has been keeping me company this afternoon and has been kind enough to organise me some refreshments during the interval," Grandpa explained to me.

I still had no idea how she knew him or what she was doing here. Before I could articulate any response, Grandpa was already suggesting that we all have a meal at his golf club.

"Actually Grandpa, I need to speak to someone about something first. I sort of made an offer to take someone back to Edinburgh as a favour to James, but nothing has been confirmed yet. It's a bit convoluted, but a friend of a friend of a friend of a friend has been left without a lift thanks to a certain individual who tends to make plans without thinking through the consequences for everybody else."

Grandpa rolled his eyes. "Would that certain individual be the notorious Hugo by any chance?"

"How did you guess?" I rolled my eyes too.

Libby stood staring at us, "I think the 'friend of a friend of a friend' could be me!"

We all looked from one to the other perplexed. At last, I found my voice: "Do you know Hugo?"

"No, not really, but my friend is Genevieve – you met her after the Bowie concert."

"Genevieve? I did?" Then it all fell into place "*Jenny*? Genevieve! Yes, I did! *Jenny*! *Genevieve*! That's *your Jenny*? I *knew* there was something vaguely familiar about her when I met her."

"Yes, that's my friend Jenny," Libby said, "I came here with her, but she didn't know that Hugo was going to be here, but when he turned up, well as you say, he makes his plans and people somehow fit in with them, but I found a nice shaded spot here and have had a *very* nice afternoon, being taught all about a game of sport that I knew nothing about at all. My day has been enriched and all the better for meeting Phillip, sorry your grandfather. During the drinks interval, I met up with Jenny and Hugo and it turns out that they will be guests of the Earl this evening so will be staying over. Hugo said that he would arrange my transport back tonight. I assumed that it would be a taxi of some sort. I had no idea that he would be begging complete strangers to take me back to Edinburgh. I feel terrible that you have been roped into this!"

"No, not at all, I couldn't be more delighted that you're the friend of a friend of a friend of my friend! I only hope that Grandpa here has put in a good word for me!"

"Well, this is wonderful news Timothy. Since you don't have to rush off, we can have a meal at the Club then you can see me into my taxi and take this lovely young lady back to Edinburgh."

❖ ❖ ❖

The journey back to Edinburgh was much too short. Libby was such good fun with a great sense of humour, and we laughed all the way back to Tollcross where I dropped her off.

"Well, you really are a knight in shining armour, thank you so much for the lift, Tim. I'm really pleased that you turned out to be the friend of a friend who was roped into rescuing me!"

"The pleasure was all mine Miss Libby, and there was absolutely no roping me into this at all. Do you fancy meeting up again, perhaps we could go for a coffee? The Pancake Place does pretty good coffee and I've discovered that I'm addicted to their pancakes with maple syrup. It would be a mercy mission really, helping to feed my addiction!"

She laughed and smiled her lovely smile. "Well if you put it that way, then how can I refuse? Do you have a number I can call you on? My landlady is a wee bit funny with men calling the flat."

I scribbled my number on a scrap of paper I found in my pocket. "It really was great meeting you again you know, and I can't wait for you to help me feed my addiction!"

She gave me a grin and a quick peck on the cheek then before I knew it, she had disappeared into her flat.

# Part 2

# 5
# Libby – Cupar, August, 1983

My mum was due to go into hospital for an operation, so I was going back home to Cupar after work on Friday and was taking a couple of days' holiday on Monday and Tuesday to stay with her. I hadn't stopped thinking about Tim since he dropped me off on Sunday, but I hadn't phoned him yet. I thought I would phone him from home after the weekend when it was quiet but for the meantime, it would be nice to catch up with my mum.

I had been feeling a bit guilty as I hadn't been home for a few months, but we spoke on the phone every Sunday. We weren't the clingy sort of family that needed to be in contact every day and my parents didn't insist that I call them, they just wanted me to get on with my life and didn't want to hold me back.

As a child I remember feeling how ancient they were – they seemed so much older than any of my friends' parents and set in their ways. They would be content to sit and watch TV in the evening, but they always encouraged me to be more adventurous. They had me later in life than they would have wanted, I think they had struggled to have children initially, then Mum had a very difficult pregnancy and childbirth and wasn't able to have any more children after me. So, it was just the three of us, a small family unit, me with my slightly ageing parents.

Don't get me wrong, we were very close, and I knew if I needed help, my parents would be first in line. But they encouraged me to be as independent as possible from an early age. I think that's how I had the courage to go to Edinburgh, because I knew that there was always a safety net there to catch me if ever I needed one.

I remember in my younger days when the world seemed too difficult for my naïve emotions to navigate without steering into some traumatic episode or another, I would stop Mum in her tracks, in whatever task she was doing and say, "Can we talk?" The answer was always yes, and we always headed for the bathroom since it was the only place where we could be assured privacy and a locked door. Not that there were any secrets in our tiny family I'm sure, but my teenage angst just needed the reassurance of privacy. I would sit perched on the loo with the toilet seat down, my mum on the wicker bathroom chair, I would pour my heart out to Mum, whilst she doled out her endless wisdom or cajoling in whatever form she felt necessary until the emotional crisis had been resolved. Even now, the smell of Imperial Leather soap takes me back to sitting talking to my mum in the little family bathroom. I was looking forward to talking to Mum this weekend and maybe telling her about Tim. It was always good to hear her perspective on things.

When I got home on Friday night, I hadn't realised just how much pain my mum had been in. She could barely walk more than three steps without having to stop. I didn't really understand what the operation would entail, but because she had been so matter-of-fact about it, I had assumed it was fairly minor. She was to be admitted to Ninewells Hospital in Dundee on Sunday evening, prior to her surgery the following morning.

The weekend flew by and before we knew it, Sunday evening had arrived and we were crossing the Tay Bridge, on our way to Ninewells Hospital.

❖❖❖

She was admitted to the ward following a series of lengthy admissions procedures then put to bed, now correctly labelled: *Mrs Maisie Fraser* with her date of birth and hospital number on a plastic wristband.

The doctor, Mr MacFadden, who was in charge of Mum's case and who would be carrying out the surgery, explained the surgery was for something called *spinal stenosis.* It turned out that the bones in her spinal canal were narrowing, and the spaces between the bones were getting smaller and smaller, compressing the nerves inside the canal. Mr MacFadden explained to us that because the nerves were being pinched, it was causing the pain to travel down her legs.

There was a lot of information for Mum to take in but typically for Mum, the two things she picked up on were the fact that she might be constipated because of the pain relief she would be given, and that she might have to have a catheter. She was always very embarrassed by anything to do with toilet functions, so I tried to get her to focus on what else was being explained. It seemed very important that she should be concentrating on what she was being told about deep breathing exercises and moving about as soon as she was able to after the surgery, but she was definitely more concerned about her bladder and bowels.

I thought Dad would want a few minutes alone with Mum before we had to leave so I made the excuse of needing to go to the ladies. When I got back to the ward, they were holding hands and Dad was gazing at Mum with such fondness and love that it melted my heart. To have spent so many years together and to still have those feelings for each other was just inconceivable. They were role models to be sure, and a hard act to follow. I wondered if I would ever find anyone I could feel this way about and fleetingly thought about Tim but brushed the thought aside thinking that I shouldn't tempt fate or get ahead of myself.

It felt like I was intruding on a beautiful, intimate moment, my heels sounding abnormally loud on the lino as I approached the bed. Dad straightened up, and squeezed Mum's hand with both of his, giving her a quick peck on the cheek as he did, hardly able to take his eyes from her.

"Now then," Mum said turning towards me, "don't let that young laddie you were telling me about distract you from your work. The last thing I want to see is you being left high and dry with no career to fall back on!"

"Of course I won't Mum, what do you take me for?" I said, then realised how irritable I sounded, so added with a laugh. "You just look after yourself and don't give these nurses any trouble!" I gave her a big hug and whispered in her ear, "Love you Mum."

"Love you too, Elizabeth, and look after your dad for me!"

❖❖❖

We waited all day on Monday to hear how the surgery had gone. Apparently, Mum's operation had been delayed so she ended up much later on the surgery list than she should have been. By the time the nurse had called to say that she was out of surgery and back in the ward, visiting hours for the evening had just started. We were reassured by the nurse that she was comfortable, but that she had received a lot of pain relief so was sleeping and probably wouldn't be up to receiving visitors this evening. "You can speak to the surgeon tomorrow if you have any questions," the nurse said, "but to be honest, Mr MacFadden does prefer to speak to his patients directly rather than the family, so it would be best to wait until visiting time tomorrow when he should be out of theatre. Mrs Fraser should be awake and any questions that she has can be answered directly to her."

We called the ward the next morning and the report was that Mum had spent a comfortable night considering the procedure she had undertaken. The nurse was quite brusque, but I assumed that it was a busy time of the morning. I didn't feel confident enough to question her any further so asked the nurse to send our love to Mrs Fraser from her husband and her daughter and that we would see her at visiting time.

At afternoon visiting time, we found that Mum had been moved to a side room. Despite the fact that she had tubes coming out of the back of her hands, she looked reasonably comfortable, and she was sleeping. Again, we were told that this was due to the side effects of the drugs given to her for the pain. I also noticed that there was a tube leading from the bed down to a stand on the floor with a plastic bag attached to it. There was a small amount of yellow liquid in the bag: a catheter, she would be mortified!

A nurse came in to check on her. She picked up the chart that was at the end of her bed and saw me looking at the catheter bag.

"Don't worry about the catheter, it's just because Mrs Fraser hasn't managed to pass any urine by herself yet. It will make her a bit more comfortable if she passes urine through this tube and stop her from getting urinary retention."

I nodded. Dad was obviously embarrassed and coughed.

"So, er…" Dad began changing the subject, "we were told that we could speak to Mr MacFadden today, is he available now."

"I'm afraid not, Mr Fraser," the nurse said, "Mr MacFadden is still in theatre at the moment, and he won't be available until later this evening. I can leave a message for him to give you a call if you like?"

"That's very kind of you dear, thank you if you could, I'd be very grateful."

We stayed for a little longer, but then the nurses came in again to change Mum's position, so we decided to leave early as Mum still hadn't woken up sufficiently to speak to us, and if we left now, we would avoid rush hour over the Tay Bridge.

❖❖❖

By the time we got home, the phone that sits in our front hall was ringing. "Damn, I missed the bloody call," said Dad. "I bet that was Mr MacFadden out of surgery." Dad so rarely used any swear words I could tell how anxious he was.

"Don't worry Dad, I'll make us a cup of tea and if he hasn't phoned back, then we can give the hospital a call."

A few minutes later though, our phone was ringing again. Dad sat on the padded seat of the old style 1970s teak telephone console table and answered in his usual telephone voice with our telephone number:

"Cupar, 960575. Yes, this is Mr Fraser.

Yes…

I, y…

Wh…I…"

He looked at me as the handset dropped to his lap and kept trying to speak.

"I…

He…said…

Your…"

Dad shook his head and his chin dropped to his chest.

I could hear whoever was on the phone, saying, "Hello, Mr Fraser, are you still there?"

I gently took the phone's handset from Dad and put my hand on his shoulder while I spoke to the doctor. As the doctor spoke, tears spilled down my cheeks. I watched my dad, my strong, dependable dad shatter to pieces. I stared in disbelief, trying to block out what the doctor was telling me. I stared at the old telephone console table, with the neat stack of telephone directories and Yellow Pages; the coiled telephone wire that kinked so badly from stretching that it didn't quite go back into position; the old carpet, threadbare from years of wear around the area of the phone; the spider plant that somehow managed to thrive from what little sunlight filtered through the glass of the front door. I stared, trying hard to block out the words, but the words just would not go away, and the tears fell.

❖ ❖ ❖

*Pulmonary embolism* was the cause of death. It was written on Mum's death certificate. There was a blood clot, probably starting in one of her legs. She had just spent too long in bed before and after the surgery, not walking or moving her legs enough, so blood couldn't circulate properly. They said that the clot must have broken loose and moved through the bloodstream and got stuck in her lung. From there, the clot would have caused too much pressure in the arteries that ran between her heart and her lungs, making her heart work too hard. The strain on her the heart was too much and her heart just failed.

❖ ❖ ❖

The next few weeks passed in a blur. The surge of adrenaline that had taken over, pushed me, and pushed me. I was either frantically cleaning everything or batch cooking until midnight. I had called my boss Mr Galbraith at the bank and they had given me a week off as compassionate leave. I had also asked if I could take another week as holiday and then I could think about my situation. Mr Galbraith had been very sympathetic and had agreed and also organised some flowers on behalf of the bank which was very kind of him.

Dad and I organised the funeral between us with the help of the local undertakers. Whilst we went through the functions required of us and made the decisions that were necessary to ensure a dignified funeral, we were merely soulless automatons, lost within our own grief. At the very time we most needed comfort from each other, instead of comfort, all we found was an unbreachable wall of grief between us as we struggled on silently, unable to console one another over our loss. Dad had lost his partner of 25 years and I had lost my anchor, my confidante, and my safety net overnight. It was a bleak, dark time for us both but finally on the morning of the funeral, we reached out to each other and for the first time in over a week, we allowed the other to see the pain we had been trying not to show. The wall of grief was breached, and the comforting hug got us through the next few hours of the funeral, knowing that we were there for each other.

The small family funeral was touching and heart-warming, with some beautiful memories and tributes from our family and friends. I felt truly blessed to have this remarkable person as my mum. Dad was very stoic and dignified as I would have expected. He engaged with everyone at the funeral, even if he didn't know them and made them feel that he understood their loss. I watched him from across the room: this was my lovely dad, the strong, brave, dependable, kind-hearted man who brought me up. He was looking at me over my auntie's head as he gave her a hug and our eyes met. He smiled encouragingly and I nodded back, acknowledging that I was doing OK. We got through the day and at the end of it all, he asked me to sit down with him for a talk.

"We've barely been able to speak to each other since your mum died Libby, we've been so wrapped up in our own grief, but I couldn't have got through this without you – you know that don't you?"

I was about to say something, but he held up his hand and continued:

"I need to say this Libby and it's hard for me so don't stop me. I love you being here with me and helping me out, you've been an absolute blessing being here, but this is not the place where you should be now, you're young and you have your own life to live so I won't be expecting you to be staying here, do you understand? That's not to say I won't enjoy you visiting me from time to time as you always have done, but you need to get yourself back to Edinburgh, or further afield if you want – the world is your oyster. It's what your mum would have wanted. Do you remember the last thing your mum said to you? She wanted you to have a career, not settle down too early and spend the rest of your life in a wee town like this."

"Your mum and I loved each other very much and I will miss her terribly. There's nothing that can bring her back, especially not you being here, wasting your potential, there's so little for you here. So do what your mum – and I – want for you and live your life."

I don't think I'd ever heard my dad say so many words in such a short space of time. He never was one for speeches. I was overwhelmed with everything, and the tears just spilled down my cheeks for the umpteenth time that day.

"Dad, the last thing Mum said to me was 'look after your dad for me' – how can I do that if I disappear off back to Edinburgh?"

"Love, you'll be looking after me by achieving your potential. Believe it or not, I am capable of looking after myself! I might need a bit of a hand with some ironing from time to time, but I might be able to get someone in to help with that. The main thing is, that if you give up everything that we know you can achieve, then what have I got to live for? If you come back here and end up throwing everything away, then I might as well just throw the towel in as well. We both want what's best for you and we all know that not going to be found with you moving back into your childhood bedroom."

I wrapped my arms around him in a big hug.

"I understand everything you have said Dad, and I appreciate all the encouragement and support that you and Mum have always given me. I have always felt that I am invincible with your support, and I will get back on my feet, but for now, I just need to be here for a bit longer, where everything is just comfortable and familiar. I won't throw anything away and I will work hard to be the best I can be, whatever that might be."

"Whatever that might be Libby, just fulfil your potential, we're not asking for anything more."

❖❖❖

# 6
# Libby – Edinburgh, October, 1983

In the end, I spent six weeks in Cupar with my dad. It took a lot longer to sort through Mum's stuff than we expected. We were doing OK. We had sad days and better days, but we were working through our grief in our own way. I was taking a big step now though and was on the train back to Edinburgh.

I had been in touch with my Landlady, Phyllis (or Phyll as she preferred to be called) who was surprisingly empathetic and said I could keep my room if I paid half my rent. Dad helped me out with the rent, so I didn't have the upheaval of a move.

Mr Galbraith, however, was not able to hold my job for me but had guaranteed an excellent reference, so I had sent my CV off to a number of job vacancies and had secured a job with the Royal Bank of Scotland in the corporate banking typing pool on a slightly higher grade because of my experience. At the interview, I had also enquired about the possibility of completing corporate banking exams, so I was ready to start my new career.

I had tried to phone Tim a couple of times but every time I tried; I got a number unobtainable tone.

I had too much on my plate right now anyway, perhaps I should take Mum's advice and concentrate on my career. I could hear Mum's voice in my head saying, "Don't let that young laddie you were telling me about distract you from your work. The last thing I want to see is you being left high and dry with no career to fall back on!" I smile, thinking about her again, blinking away the tears that always seem to be too ready to surface.

The train slowed down and we were pulling into Haymarket. I could always tell when Edinburgh was getting close because of the smell of malt and yeast in the air from the breweries. Waverley would be next, so I started gathering my belongings together ready to exit the train quickly.

The early evenings were darker now, than when I left Edinburgh in August and much colder, and with my heavy suitcase, I couldn't face a bus ride back to Tollcross so I hailed a taxi.

Back at the flat, Phyll welcomed me home with a cup of tea and a pile of letters, telling me that she'd taken the liberty of cleaning my room for me and changing my sheets. She really was very kind-hearted.

"I'm so sorry to hear about your mum. If there's anything you need, or if you need a bit of company just give my door a knock. You don't want to be sitting here all by yourself feeling lonely."

She gave me a warm smile and patted my shoulder then left me to sort myself out.

I settled back into my room and started to unpack. It did feel cold and lonely in Edinburgh, and I was tempted to knock on my landlady's door, but instead I looked at the pile of letters. Among the usual bank statements and uninteresting post, there was a card from Jenny and a hand-written envelope that looked intriguing. Inside was a condolence card and a letter from Tim.

*30th August 1983*

*Dear Libby,*

*I am so sorry to hear of the untimely death of your mother, please accept my deepest and sincere condolences for your terrible loss. If I could do anything at all that could alleviate your grief, I would be honoured to be of help.*

*You may of course be wondering how I am aware of this news, but I have to say that I was so desperate to hear from you that I had to ask a 'friend of a friend of a friend' if they had heard from you. I was told of your news and of course that you had left Edinburgh for the foreseeable future and that they did not know when you would be returning. I am writing this and sending it in the hope that you do in fact return to Edinburgh and read this. It was so wonderful to finally meet you at the Charity Cricket match, and I have not stopped thinking about you since. I would dearly love to see you again.*

*I do hope that you are recovering from your loss and that I will hear from you again soon.*

*With fondest regards.*
*Tim,*
*Telephone: Edinburgh 496 0172*

I smiled to myself at the formality of Tim's letter. It was quite endearing and seemed completely at odds with his playful sense of humour that he revealed on the short car journey from Haddington to Edinburgh. I suppose the whole aspect of death can do that to people, they don't know what to say or how to say it, so they fall back to their tried and tested formulae and phrases and try not to offend the bereaved.

But what would I want him to have said? If he had written "I know you're hurting Libby, and I want to wrap my arms around you until all the hurt goes away" would I have welcomed it, or would I have run a mile from him? I hardly knew him really. Did I honestly want to get into a relationship right now with everything else that was going on? I'd just lost my mum, I was starting a new job, possibly working towards a new banking career. I wasn't sure I was in the right place emotionally to open myself up to all the angst that came with a new relationship as well.

Anyway, he'd given me his number again, so he was making sure I still had it. Thinking about this, I fished out the scribbled number he had given me previously and looked at the phone number on the letter. I laughed to myself and thought silently that this was definitely a doctor in the making, with a ready-made doctor's handwriting. The digits 1 and 7 were virtually identical on his scribbled note. I had been dialling 0772 instead of 0172. No wonder I kept getting a number unobtainable tone!

Just then Phyllis knocked on my door.

"Libby, your dad's on the phone, I thought you might want to take it."

"Thanks, Phyll, I'm just coming."

I knew Phyllis didn't like me taking calls so this was definitely over and above what she would normally do for me.

"Hi Dad, how are you? Yes, just got in, not a bad journey thanks, and Phyllis has been really kind to me and has kept my room fresh and clean so everything was ready for me to come back to. Yes, I'll be OK. I'll be thinking of you though. Yes, I'll call you tomorrow from the phone box. Love you, Dad. Yes, love you, bye Dad, Bye."

I put down the receiver and closed my eyes, trying to keep the tears from falling. Just hearing his voice made me want to jump on the train straight back to Cupar. I took a deep breath and shouted so Phyllis could hear through the door: "Thanks, Phyll, Dad just wanted to make sure I got back OK. Just a quick call."

"Rightio, not a problem," she called back.

Back in my room I finished unpacking. I had brought back some new photographs of Mum and Dad and some family photos too. My room had a more homely feel once I'd finished and felt less cold and unwelcoming. As I was working on my room, I had been thinking about what Dad had said. I really needed to make this work out, I didn't want to end up back in Cupar, even if I was working in the local bank there. I felt that my life was leading me further afield, I just didn't quite know where yet.

❖❖❖

# 7
# Tim – Edinburgh, June, 1984

It took me a while to stop thinking about Libby – I used to call her the girl with the lovely big eyes. I was definitely smitten with her! I had given her my number twice, but she hadn't called me, so I guess it wasn't me that she was interested in. It was a shame really because the time that we did meet and really did manage to talk, we got on so well together. And she spent a long time talking to Grandpa too and he thought she was delightful.

Such is life I suppose! It was the end of $3^{rd}$ year, and the exams were over, thank God. Charles and I were parting company in terms of being flat mates so I was driving 'home' to spend the summer with Grandpa in the large family home near Berwick upon Tweed, and had organised a flat share with some other less raucous and more studious friends for the next academic year.

I still had two more years to go at medical school followed by a two-year foundation programme before I could practice. Admittedly I could practice while I was in my foundation programme, but this would have to be supervised. Then after my foundation programme I would need to do my core medical training and then think about what speciality I would go into with even more training. I was still considering paediatric psychiatry, but I wasn't sure if that was the right direction for me in view of my own history. But regardless of which direction I chose, I definitely didn't need someone like Charles keeping me back with late nights and disturbed sleep if I was going to get where I wanted to go.

The drive wasn't too long and hopefully wouldn't take me more than an hour and a half. I bought a bottle of water and a packet of Polo's when I filled up with petrol and had the radio to keep me company so was all set to go. I was still driving the extremely old Fiesta that was given to me (second hand) when I passed my driving test at the age of 18, so the in-car entertainment system was very poor. The radio only had a few pre-set buttons that actually worked: one long-wave pre-set button and a couple of medium-wave pre-set buttons, the spring on the others had gone so wouldn't stay connected.

Radio 1 was currently playing on medium-wave and 11:00 o'clock on a weekday morning meant it was time for *Our Tune* and for Simon Bates to start his long, dramatic monologue, telling the eager listeners about some poor sod's dismal love life with the theme tune from Franco Zeffirelli's Romeo and Juliet playing mournfully in the background. On and on the tale went! God it was dreary! Then it was time for their *special song* to be played. This time though, the story that was being told was so conflicted that I couldn't imagine what on earth the song could actually be! The violins of Rota's Love Theme were reaching the final few bars so the listeners would be poised for the reveal of *Our Tune*.

Then it started.

I recognised the song from the opening bars: *I'm Not in Love* by 10CC. I immediately froze, the music taking me straight back to 1975 and boarding school. In my mind, I could smell the strong pine disinfectant, the smell of the school locker rooms, mixed with the smell of mud, boots and acrid adolescent sweat.

The music played on, and the memory of that awful day replayed itself in my mind: of the day I was left broken and tormented in the locker room with the taunt of "*big boys don't cry*" echoing as the door was slammed shut.

Now as I was driving, the feeling started with a tightening in my gut, rising through to my chest and I felt my heart rate rise. I felt like there was a cold vice around my head and neck, there was pounding in my ears and my carotid pulse was throbbing; sweat was running down my temples and my chest: I had to pull over. Someone behind me blasted their horn and overtook me as I slowed down. Somehow, I managed to steer the car to the kerb and park it safely, if somewhat haphazardly and switched off the engine and the radio.

I recognised that I was having a panic attack and knew that I shouldn't try to fight it. I grabbed at the paper bag beside me containing the bottled water and the Polo's and emptied it so that I could use the bag to help regulate my breathing. I also knew that I needed to put back some carbon dioxide into my body and balance the oxygen flow, so I took deep slow breaths and tried to focus on more positive images, telling myself that it would pass.

After several minutes of deep and calming breaths, I had recovered sufficiently to look around me and get my bearings. I gave myself a few more minutes, drank some water and made sure I was fully recovered. I hadn't had a flashback like that for a while but at least I had managed the panic attack and got through it.

I checked my radial pulse; it had returned to normal. I felt calm again so restarted the engine and switched the radio back on, deciding to try long-wave. I was pleased to find I'd missed the shipping forecast and that Test Match Special had started on Radio 4, that would be a good distraction for me, let's hope that England would do a better job at Edgbaston against the West Indies in the test series than they did in the One Day Internationals.

I'd arrived in Berwick to hear Grandpa through his open window bewail the loss of yet another England wicket – it really wasn't looking good for the English batsmen. If Grandma had still been around, she would have been rolling her eyes; I took a moment and felt comforted by thoughts of my childhood memories. Grandma's warm smile and sparkling eyes, even when she was trying to be stern with Grandpa, that's how I remembered her most. It was good to be back, but there was still a big part of me that felt the loss of Grandma, it must be especially difficult for Grandpa, being in the big family home without her. The house was well staffed so he had a lot of help but he must have been lonely without her.

"Poor show for this England side," Grandpa said cheerily as he came out to greet me on the vast driveway. "Far too many wickets before lunch. I think we may have thrown this one away already! Anyway, my boy, good to see you, how was the journey? I'll get Hamish to take those bags to your room shall I, then we can have lunch."

I was a little taken aback, I was so used to having to do things for myself that I hadn't dreamt of getting someone else to take my bags to my old bedroom.

"Don't worry Gramps, I'll take them up now if that's OK, then I can see my old room and freshen up at the same time. I'll only be five minutes."

After lunch we spent a companionable afternoon, watching England being demolished by the West Indies and we talked well into the evening before Grandpa finally admitted defeat himself stating he was heading off to bed, I followed suit and was out like a light.

❖ ❖ ❖

I am gripped by a terror that I have never experienced before: the pain is unbearable, excruciating. I can't breathe, I can't move, I can't shout for help. I am being crushed by the weight of him. His voice is in my ear, taunting me. His breath with the stench of stale cigarettes makes me want to vomit. I smell blood, sweat, disinfectant, all mingled with the smell of his breath. Tears spring to my eyes. He is taunting me.

*"Big boys don't cry."*

I look down and see a stray rugby boot covered in mud wondering who it belongs to, my mind trying to escape from the present.

*"Big boys don't cry."*
*"Shhh…"*

I wake up in a state of confusion, sweat has pooled at the hollow at the base of my neck, I'm groggy with sleep and my mouth is dry.

Grandpa is beside me, a concerned look on his face.

"Still having those nightmares, my boy?"

He offers me a glass of water and helps me to drink it, not really expecting an answer from me. He has never pushed me to talk about my emotions, but he was the most caring man I knew. I have had far more affection from him than I have had from my own father.

"Thanks Gramps, yes just a bad dream. I'll be fine though."

"Good man, just call if you need anything, you know I'm a light sleeper."

He rested his hand on my shoulder and locked his eyes on mine. The exchange was so affectionate it nearly brought tears to my eyes. Grandpa really was better than a father to me.

He was the only one who knew that I had *those nightmares.* They obviously started after the incident back at boarding school. The physical injury was bad enough, but the mental and physical trauma had stayed with me for many years, and I had never really stopped feeling the shame and humiliation. I still wonder now why I hadn't been able to stop the incident from happening or run away, or called for help, why was I so weak that day? I used to wake up with nightmares regularly, but I hadn't had one for a few years now. It must have been triggered by that song, and the flashback I had earlier.

❖❖❖

# 8
# Tim – Boarding School, 1975

I wasn't really enjoying being at boarding school. I missed Mama of course, and I hadn't seen Grandpa for months. I missed Grandpa most of all. Father said it would be the making of me. He had also boarded at this school and naturally he was Head Boy and Games Captain, so I had a lot to live up to.

I enjoyed sport: cricket was my favourite mainly because I always used to watch it with Grandpa. He was the one who taught me how the scoring system worked. It was quite complex, but he made it so interesting and exciting. I could bowl a decent over and I was a fast runner over short distances, so I was selected for the Junior First XI even though some people thought I was a bit on the small side. Grandpa was delighted. It barely registered on father's radar.

The first year was quite lonely; it was odd being in a dorm with other boys, getting used to their noises at night and their peculiar routines. There was a particular smell about the dorm – the fetid smell of adolescence mixed with the heady smell of layers of lavender wood polish that clung to your clothes for days into the school holidays.

The school, like most schools, was segregated into competitive Houses. Each of these were 'ruled' by House Masters and deputised with an even firmer hand by the older boys. In the enormous dark wood-panelled dining hall, you knew exactly what the pecking order was, because the higher up the pecking order you were, the further away you were from the House Masters on the long refectory tables. The House Master sat at the head of each table, with his deputy at the other end, the youngest boys being closest to the masters for supervision.

I had made a good friend, James, in my first year, and we became inseparable, so life was not completely unbearable. We soon realised though that everybody in the school was to be given a nickname of some sort. We had escaped our re-branding so far, but we knew it wouldn't be long before one of the older boys would find something to mock us about and taunt us with, then turn that into our nickname. We even talked about giving ourselves a nickname to pre-empt the inevitable but had a surprisingly insightful, grown-up discussion about how these names could change people's perceptions of that person from something positive to something negative. So, we waited in trepidation, knowing that our day would come soon enough, when one of the domineering, overbearing older boys who seemed to be in control of these things would find some flaw in our character to assign a vulgar nickname that would taunt us for the rest of our school days.

At the end of the school year, we had an inter-house games tournament. I was 12-years old at the time and small for my age but because of my speed over a short distance I was picked for the 100 meters for my House. I came in second place and was really pleased with my performance. I'm sure father would have preferred me to have come in first place, but this was not really my sport, so I was happy to have picked up the silver.

The atmosphere was good humoured and light-hearted in the locker rooms and there was a lot of chatter and laughter as we all bundled and splashed our way through the communal showers. We were only halfway through our ablutions when a loud, booming voice was heard: "Shift it kids, make way for the big boys."

Lance was an older boy – a bully and large for his age, already growing facial and body hair and his voice had broken, he was loud and brash with it. He was 14 but already quite manly in stature. Most of the younger boys tried to avoid him if they possibly could because he was a nasty piece of work.

Unfortunately, I was closest to Lance as he entered the communal shower.

"What have we got here then lads," he boomed, looking me up and down "I think we've caught ourselves a little tiddler." He roared with laughter at his own joke and made to grab at my still underdeveloped genitals. Horrified and humiliated I swiped at Lance's hand, pushing it away, trying simultaneously to turn away and cover myself up. Enraged, Lance pushed me over and I landed on my back, my genitals on display for everyone to see.

Lance's voice boomed against the tiled walls and carried down the length of the communal shower: "Has anyone ever seen such a little tiddler? What do you think, Tiddler? That's a good name for you don't you think, Tiddler?"

Lance's entourage were now behind me laughing and jeering "Tiddler, Tiddler." I scrambled to my feet and pushed past the silent and petrified younger boys as I staggered down the length of the shower away from Lance and the older boys, my face scarlet, seething with anger and embarrassment. I knew that I would have been given a nickname at some time but this could not have been worse. How could I ever live this one down? I also knew that this would hang over me for the rest of my days at school. I could feel tears prick my eyes but did not dare cry. I had to hold it together until I got back to my dorm.

James tried to talk to me about it later that day, but I just shut him out. It was something that I needed to keep compartmentalised in the deepest recesses of my mind; concealed and obscured from my fragile emotions so I could hide from the shame and humiliation I felt.

❖ ❖ ❖

Over the summer holidays I had been staying with Grandpa. It was so good to be away from boarding school and to be back in my familiar space. Grandpa and I spent as much time as possible together to make up for the lost weeks. We watched local cricket matches, where I honed my scoring to perfection. We went for walks along the Berwickshire coastal paths where we had long talks amongst other things about his time in the RAF, World War II, Nazi Germany and the Holocaust – topics that still haunted him three decades on. We still talked a lot about Grandma. It had been two years since she had died, it had been a very sad time and it still made me sad when I thought about her.

It was on one of our clifftop walks when we stopped at our favourite spot, looking out onto the rugged North Sea, Grandpa was silent for a while, then in his quiet gentle voice that somehow gave no scope for denial he said: "I sense a deep sadness in you since the last time I saw you Tim, and I wonder what might have happened to you to make you so unhappy."

I said nothing for several minutes, not looking at Grandpa, but out to sea. I allowed my mind to delve deep into the recesses once again, to the humiliation of that day. The tears that I had held back for all those weeks finally sprang to my eyes and rolled down my cheeks and my nose. Grandpa silently gave me his neatly folded handkerchief and nodded, waiting patiently.

I poured out the whole embarrassing incident to Grandpa who was outraged. He asked me if I wanted him to have a word with the headmaster. I begged him not to – I could only imagine what would happen if word got out that I had asked my grandfather to intervene. Grandpa was very distressed about the whole nickname ritual and couldn't understand why father would send me to a school where he knew that sort of thing went on. Being my maternal grandfather, he didn't have the same allegiance to the school as Father did.

"But why are people so cruel to each other, Grandpa? Why do bullies want to belittle you so much and make you feel so bad about yourself?"

"It's hard to say Tim, there are many reasons why people bully. It's likely that this Lance boy has been bullied himself, or he may be insecure himself, and bullying others gives him more power and makes him feel more secure. The one thing I want you to remember though is this: when people try to belittle you and devalue you, in no way should you *believe* that you are in anyway of less value. It is merely something that is done to you by another person it is not something that is inherent in you. Think of the way that Nazi Germany devalued the Jewish community: millions of good, kind, decent human beings were persecuted and killed, not because of anything inherent in them but because of something that was done to them by a group of people with more power."

I thought about this for a while, about the millions of people from the Jewish community who had lost their lives because one person influenced another group of people and their power had devastated that community. It did bear a similarity to the way bullies operated, but made my own experience feel trivial in comparison. My own predicament paled into insignificance when I considered the suffering that these people had to endure for years at the hands of the Nazi regime.

Over the summer break, we talked about this more and considered how I might respond to the other boys if, or rather when, they approached me using this nickname. I reassured Grandpa that I would be OK now that I had talked to him about it and that I would just try and shrug it off and get through the next few years until it was over – as Grandpa himself had said, it was just a name that an insecure boy had used to make himself feel more powerful. I was no less valued as a result. Nevertheless, I was very anxious when the summer holidays were over, and the new school year had started.

❖ ❖ ❖

My worst fears had been realised and my new nickname *Tiddler Ashford* had spread like wildfire down the corridors and dorms of the boarding school. I tried not to react to it as I had rehearsed with Grandpa and merely shrugged my shoulders or shook my head in what I hoped was giving a disappointed look.

I had James to support me, and he was a rock, he was also very impressed by how I handled everything. I told him that I had spent weeks talking it through with Grandpa and how much it had helped. The whole thing was getting waring though I had to admit.

We had been back in school for a few months and an extra tuck box had arrived from Grandpa, it was reminiscent of my time at prep school when gifts from my grandparents used to arrive. I was given permission to collect it and take it back to my dorm but then had to rush to get to the boys locker rooms – I was late for rugby practice but had a permission slip so I wouldn't be penalised. I ran into the boys' locker room and heard a strange grunting, almost animal-like noise. I turned around and stared, at first not quite understanding what I was seeing. Then with shocking clarity I realised that I had interrupted Lance in a blatant sexual act with another boy. The other boy quickly pulled up his trousers and ran out of the locker room, so I didn't see who it was. Lance, was furious and turned towards me with his booming voice:

"What the fuck are you doing here Tiddler Ashford you little pervert? I'll teach you to snoop where you're not wanted. You think you can snoop around here and spy on me, you little pervert. I'll show you what happens to perverts."

Before I could move, Lance had grabbed hold of me and spun me around pinning my arms against me using one strong arm, his other arm free, my back was towards him. I couldn't move I was so terrified; I was literally paralysed with fear. I wanted to run or shout out for help but I just couldn't move. I could feel his free hand in my trousers and in my shorts. I was mortified, disgusted, but still I could not move or call out for help.

"I'm not sure I could do anything with this little tiddler," he laughed grabbing at my penis.

My mortification grew deeper but still could not say or do anything, I was frozen to the spot with fear. Lance takes this as compliance and pulls down my trousers and shorts.

"You like this don't you, you're not saying *'no'* to me are you? You *are* a little pervert, aren't you?" He penetrates me, tearing my anus, I am in excruciating pain as he thrusts himself into me again and again. I can smell his nicotine breath mixed with the acrid adolescent sweat emanating from his body: the combination of pain and the smell from him makes me want to vomit.

When he is done, Lance grabs me by the hair on the base of my neck and growls gruffly in my ear: "You tell anybody about this and there will be worse than that, do you understand?" I snivel and try to nod but am barely able to move, still frozen by fear.

"And you can stop that snivelling too – remember: big boys don't cry."

He walked away shouting *"Big boys don't cry..."* mimicking the words of the 10CC song that had been playing on the radio all summer.

I am left alone, I curl up in a foetal position on the floor, shaking now and cold. I try to move, try to pull my shorts back into place but they are ripped and wet with blood and semen. They disgust me, I feel sick, I smell the pine disinfectant from the floor mingling with the smell of my shorts, and I throw up. Tears spring to my eyes and I am sobbing, alone, in pain and terrified. I hear footsteps coming towards me and my fear intensifies. I don't have the energy to move so I cover my head with my arms, shaking and sobbing, not able to take any more pain or humiliation.

"Good God man what has happened to you?"

I let out my breath, not realising that I had been holding it. It was the games master, Mr Jones. I don't know how long I had been sitting there, but just then I heard the bell for the next period so it must have been nearly an hour. I could hear the noise of boys coming bustling into the locker rooms but thankfully Mr Jones took charge and shouted to everyone to get outside and he locked the doors behind them.

Coming back towards me but giving me space, he said to me:

"Who did this to you Ashford?" Then when there was no response, more gently:

"Tim, lad, who did this to you."

I could not speak for gulping for air and sobbing.

"Right, first things first, let's get Matron to come and see you."

I was taken by stretcher, covered with a blanket to the small sick bay, there were only three beds in each of the two small wards and thankfully none of the other beds were occupied. There were lots of rumours flying around but it was generally accepted by all that I had an accident in the locker room.

❖❖❖

With only a few more weeks of term left, it was agreed that I should be cared for at home. This actually meant returning to my grandparents' house in Scotland because father had a three-month contract in Singapore and Mama had joined him. This pleased me immensely and I couldn't imagine a better place to recuperate. And quite honestly, I couldn't cope with being with the other boys, being stared at, being talked about, being the boy who was buggered by Lance.

Grandpa was the only person who I was able to talk to about the incident. He talked to the headmaster about it and Lance thankfully disappeared before the end of the term. The headmaster brushed it under the carpet and the governing body was never informed. There were some rumours and some questions, but the incident was never investigated so in the end nobody ever found out about it. I could go back to school without any of the other boys knowing what happened – *only me*.

The headmaster talked to me about it and said that had it been investigated, it would have been my evidence against Lance's and "*did I really want to go through all that again?*" His advice was to put the incident behind me.

Father never really discussed the trauma or abuse with me and just brushed it off as one of those things that happens at boarding school saying that I should just get over it. I suspected that he didn't want to be the cause of bad publicity for such a prestigious school, especially since his photograph was in the gallery of past head boys.

When I returned to school, I was very wary of people, I certainly didn't trust people easily and didn't want to befriend anyone, especially not older boys. I couldn't go into the locker room without shaking, the smell of the room, dirty socks, disinfectant, gym bags, muddy boots, all brought back memories. Each time that happened I would be sent to the sick room and Matron would talk me through the episode; her calm, quiet voice with a gentle Scottish lilt gently soothing me and helping me with calming breathing exercises.

The headmaster did make an announcement that the use of Nicknames should be stopped but it made little difference and the re-branding still went on. There were still boys who occasionally called me Tiddler throughout my time at School but I always remembered the discussion I had with Grandpa and tried not to feel devalued by the name.

❖❖❖

# 9
# Libby – September, 1988

I suppose you could call it running away, but I'd had enough of being stifled by him. I felt that I couldn't breathe without being questioned: "Where are you going? Who are you seeing? How long will you be? When will you be back?" That was bad enough, but when he started with, "You shouldn't wear this or you shouldn't eat that," I started to feel that I wasn't in control of my own life any more.

And anyway, opportunities in the male dominated world of corporate banking did not come around very often, so when a vacancy for a manager's assistant was advertised in the Birmingham branch, I made an application and kept everything crossed. I had already started my corporate banking exams with the Royal Bank of Scotland and had been making good progress, so my manager had encouraged me to apply. It was a dream come true, but after a telephone interview and a glowing reference from my manager, I was offered the job.

It had been a really difficult decision, but I'd talked it through with Dad and as usual, he encouraged me to fulfil my potential and be the best that I could be, and to remember the conversation we had after Mum had died.

"You'll only be a train ride away, Libby – it's not as though you're moving to Australia! You should do what you feel is right for you and do it while you're still young. You're still only 23 and there is so much more for you to see before you settle down. You're right not to settle for someone that doesn't make you happy. Don't waste your potential."

I had shared a flat with Davey in Edinburgh for the last 11 months. We had met at the bank and had been dating for nearly two years, but now things seemed to be going from bad to worse. One weekend when I got back from visiting Dad, I decided to tackle Davey about it. I'd popped into Marks and Sparks on Princes Street to pick up something nice for tea, but thought I should tackle the conversation first so I sat him down hoping that he'd be amenable to a discussion, but he just looked at me as critically as ever. I wondered what he was about to comment on this time: my hair was too messy or my top didn't match my skirt. It could have started with an argument, but I decided that an adult, frank discussion was the best approach.

"Davey…I…" I started, but he immediately interrupted me.

"You do realise that your train got in over an hour ago? It only takes 20 minutes to get from Waverley to here by bus and *you* took an expensive taxi. So, Libby, would you mind telling me where you have been for the last hour?"

I blinked several times, taken aback at his sudden aggression. Being adult and frank was going to be difficult when he was so angry. I felt out of my depth now, I knew he had a bit of a temper, but because he was never violent, I continued, sounding more confident than I actually felt. Wary of him though, I kept eye contact with him and said with as steady a voice as I could manage: "Davey, I am really not comfortable with the way that you speak to me like that." He made to speak again with a scornful look on his face but I held up my hand assertively and stopped him, gaining more confidence in myself as I spoke.

"In fact, Davey, when you talk to me like that, it really hurts me and makes me feel very unhappy and I have to say, I have been very unhappy for a while now. I think that you must feel the same too, or you wouldn't be so critical of me. There's not a day when there's something you think I'm doing wrong. You don't like the way I dress, you don't like my friends, you question every second I'm out of the house. I think we are both unhappy so I think we need to end the relationship now, before we make each other even more unhappy. I need to let you know that I've been offered another job, so I'm moving out of Edinburgh."

He looked at me incredulously, then the look turned darker and changed to fury. He tightened his fists, his knuckles turning white. For a moment, I became a little scared, then he seemed to calm down.

"You're right," he said.

I released a breath that I didn't know I had been holding.

"In fact, you don't know how right you are Libby," he continued in a slow, cruel, cutting voice, "You really are quite pathetic, you *don't* know how to dress, you have *no* sense of style, you have no etiquette, you certainly don't know how to treat a man."

I was stunned and for a moment speechless, then all the pent-up frustration that I had been holding back was finally unshackled and suddenly I no longer felt any ties to him: "Seriously? You are unbelievable Davey. Do you honestly think that after everything I have just said to you that this is the best response?"

There was stunned silence between us, both of us knowing that the final line had been crossed and that there was no way back in the relationship. I refused to waste any more energy on a discussion with him so just looked at him pitifully, shaking my head then turned my back on him and walked out of the room.

❖ ❖ ❖

It was a dreadful few weeks, you could cut the atmosphere in the flat with a knife, but I needed to organise my life before I left Edinburgh and moved to Birmingham and couldn't just leave straight away.

I had found a flat share for young professionals in Birmingham and paid my deposit and now everything was in place.

Dad had hired a small van and we packed all my belongings from my flat that had accumulated over the last five years of life in Edinburgh into removal boxes and crammed them into the back of the van, back to Cupar.

❖ ❖ ❖

So here I was, two months later taking the train from Cupar again, but this time changing at Edinburgh, Waverley with an onward bound journey to Birmingham. This time I was looking forward to new opportunities, a new job and a new adventure in England, feeling excited and petrified in the same way that I felt when I moved to Edinburgh, but older and wiser, with more confidence in myself and knowing that I could always come back to my safety net if things didn't work out.

Not long after we had left Waverley, engrossed in a book, I was aware of someone asking if the seat opposite me was available. Barely taking my eyes from my book, I indicated that it was indeed free.

A seemingly tall man bundled himself into the seat opposite. He appeared to take up a lot of room on the shared table between us. Even his coffee cup and croissant had been pushed towards my side, giving me no room to rest my book down. I sighed and cleared my throat, looking questioningly at the cup, hoping that he might take the hint and move it, but rather than doing anything about it, he was grinning at me.

"The last time we met, I promised you pancakes with maple syrup and coffee at the Pancake Place – I'm afraid British Rail coffee isn't up to much, but I hope that this will make up for it until I can offer you something better?"

I looked up at the man speaking to me and studied his face for the first time. A warm deep familiarity came flooding back, followed closely by a feeling of deep affection.

"Tim? Oh, my goodness! I can't believe it's you! What an amazing coincidence!"

I looked at the coffee and croissant offering and thought back to the last time we met. He did indeed invite me to the Pancake Place, I laughed at the memory, nodding at the croissant. "Yes, I do remember that, it was supposed to be a *Mercy Mission*, helping to feed your sugar addiction! How have you been all these years?"

"Well, obviously I'm still a recovering maple syrup addict, but more importantly, how are you? I was so sorry to hear about your mother."

"Thank you, yes, and thank you for the lovely letter, it was very kind of you to write."

I felt a pang of sadness as I thought back to that time, five years ago now, but I still had times when sadness crept over me and engulfed me. I shook myself mentally and brought myself back to the present.

"I did try to call you, several times. I eventually did get through and left a message with your flatmate, but when I didn't hear from you, I thought I must have left it too long. I was sorry that I wasn't able to get in touch with you Tim."

"I was never given a message from you," he replied sadly, "I am so sorry too Libby, because however long it was, it would never have been too long."

Tim held my gaze with such strong emotions that I had to look away. I swallowed back a lump in my throat, feeling overwhelmed both with grief for my mum and the memories of five years ago when I thought I might be falling for him. He was talking again, saying something humorous to lighten the atmosphere. Again, I brought myself back to the present and listened to his voice: "So however long it took I was always going to wait because I'm pinning my hopes on you helping me with my addiction, remember? So anyway, what's been happening to you over the last few years and where are you headed?"

And the five-hour journey to Birmingham New Street passed in a flash, catching up with five missed years.

# 10
# Tim – September, 1988

I was hoping to complete my speciality training in oncology and had an interview at the Queen Elizabeth Hospital in Birmingham under a prestigious consultant. It was a long way to move, but this was where the vacancy was, and it was definitely an excellent teaching hospital. My rotation in oncology, working with so many inspirational cancer patients had helped to make up my mind about the specialist route I wanted to take. Early on in my career I had considered paediatric psychiatry, but after my rotation in psychiatry, I didn't feel I had what it took. I also wondered if the flashbacks I still occasionally had would hamper my ability to help others in trauma. But if I'm totally honest, it's not that I don't think I have the ability to help others in trauma, it's just that supporting people with their emotions and traumas would be too difficult for me to deal with. Oncology was a good choice though and I did enjoy it.

My CV had gone down well as had the paper I had written: *'Palliative Oncology: Dignity and Care of the Older Woman'*. It was a paper written from the heart as well as being an academic and clinical piece, with reflections of my grandma in mind. But it had been well received in medical journals as well as by the consultant so hopefully a good interview would get me through.

I decided not to drive to Birmingham as I wasn't familiar with the route and especially not the confusing Spaghetti Junction once I got off the M6. The train from Edinburgh to Birmingham New Street was to take about five hours so I had plenty of time to brush up on interview questions on the journey.

Boarding the train at Waverley, bizarrely I thought I saw a glimpse of someone who was the double of Libby, the girl who I was head over heels with at the end of third year medical School. I hadn't thought of her for a while, but when I did, she still made my pulse race. I was kidding myself if I thought I was really over her, even after all these years. I was sitting a few seats down from *Libby's double*, who was absorbed in a book, but every time I caught a glimpse of her, I was more and more convinced that it was actually Libby.

I decided that I needed caffeine so went to the buffet car and bought what British Rail purports to pass off as black coffee and a croissant. My heart sinks as the server spoons instant coffee from a catering sized tin of instant coffee powder and adds water from an electric hot water urn, gives it a cursory stir and hands it to me. I sniff warily at the lukewarm coffee and wince at the chicory smell as I head back towards my seat.

As I get closer, I am able to observe the Libby-lookalike more clearly and there is no doubt that it is Libby. I notice that the there is a vacant seat opposite her so rather than return to my own seat, I interrupt her and ask if the seat is free.

"Go ahead," she said without looking at me or taking her eyes from her book.

I sit down noisily, and cheekily push the coffee and croissant towards her trying to get her attention, but there is still no reaction, so I push it closer. She clears her throat and looks at the coffee but says nothing. I wonder what to say to her, then remember the last time we met, I wonder if she would remember that? I clear my own throat: "The last time we met, I promised you pancakes with maple syrup and coffee at the Pancake Place – I'm afraid British Rail coffee isn't up to much, but I hope that this will make up for it until I can offer you something better?"

She looks up at me and I see her big, beautiful eyes for the first time in five years and I am flooded with emotions.

Her smile, her eyes, her laugh as she throws her head back, remembering the so-called *Mercy Mission*. I am so thrilled that she remembers me.

Then foolishly, I mention the death of her mother, and the sadness that sweeps over her is palpable. I want to wrap her in my arms and hold her; I can't bear to see her so unhappy. She tells me that she tried to leave a message. I'm trying to process this: to think I ached for her to call and spent months trying to get over the fact that she didn't; that we could have spent the last five years together. I can't take my eyes from her face; my heart is bursting with emotion. She can't hold my gaze. I'm left wondering how I could possibly fit back into her life now. I need to lighten the atmosphere; this is getting too intense. I change the subject and make a joke.

The next few hours are incredible. We are able to talk and laugh as though we last met only a week ago, without the awkwardness that might have been expected after a five-year gap. We have so much to talk about our lives and we spend a wonderful few hours catching up.

❖❖❖

I can hardly believe that she is moving to Birmingham. Could it be possible that there really are stars that align and two people get together at the right place at the right time?

We had spent a glorious five hours talking and laughing all the way to Birmingham New Street. I find out that she has already organised a flat share in an area called Selly Park which when I consult a Pocket A to Z of Birmingham that I had to foresight to buy, turns out not to be too far from the QE Hospital so we agreed to share a taxi. I helped her with her two large suitcases and bundle them into the taxi.

"You're travelling light," she indicated to my overnight bag.

"I'm taking the train back tomorrow evening," I explain, "so only needed an overnight bag."

We arrived in Selly Park, and I helped Libby with her bags. The landlord wasn't available to meet her, but the girl she was sharing with, Sandra, seemed to have everything in hand and since the taxi was waiting, I said I'd leave her to get settled in.

"Thanks for everything Tim, it was just brilliant meeting you again. It's a shame you have to go back tomorrow, or we could have had that coffee after all!"

"Well, I should be finished with the interview after lunchtime, and I'm taking the early evening train at 6:30 so I have all afternoon to kill if you fancy meeting up? I could drop by here on my way back to the city centre if you like? Probably around 2:30 tomorrow afternoon and we could find somewhere for a coffee?"

"Yes, I'd love that! I'll see you tomorrow then."

I waved as the taxi drove away and heard her shout:

"Good luck with your interview, and I hope I haven't disrupted your preparation too much!"

I hadn't given my interview preparation a thought! I would need to work all evening to go through my notes!

❖❖❖

I woke early the next morning in the room I had been allocated in the medical residence block of the QE Hospital. I had slept well considering, and felt refreshed and energised.

I was very impressed with the medical personnel department who had organised everything, and I even had a site map to help me find my way around. I made my way to the staff restaurant for breakfast, passing the consultants' dining room on the way thinking, "One day, maybe I'll be breakfasting in there!"

The interview was rigorous but fair and I felt that I had answered all their questions. I did feel quite drained afterwards though, but the thought of meeting up with Libby even for a couple of hours lightened my step.

When I got back to Libby's flat, she had already been armed with some local knowledge and suggested that we try a little cafe called *Drucker's* for coffee and cake which wasn't too far from New Street in Great Western Arcade. It was in a beautiful Grade II listed Victorian arcade that had been restored only a few years earlier with quaint shops and cafes, not at all what I would have expected in what I thought was a gritty industrial city, I certainly had a lot to learn about the heritage of this city if this was going to be my new home.

The coffee was good, and I opted for a delicious, mille-feuille: a creme patisserie and puff pastry sprinkled with lots of sugar.

Libby smiled indulgently at me, "That's definitely one way of getting your sugar fix!"

I laughed, "It definitely hits the spot! I really should know better, being a doctor, you know, but I can't resist it!"

"So, are you a qualified doctor now?"

"I am qualified, Dr Ashford at your service, but I have more years of training to do. The interview was for specialist training in oncology – specialising in diagnosing and treating cancer. It wasn't something that I had thought about until my rotation, but something just clicked."

"Grandpa was quite touched when I told him – my grandma died of cancer you see, many years ago now but he still misses her terribly."

"I can understand that, you never stop missing the people who die, you just learn to live with the fact that they are not there anymore."

She paused for a while, obviously reflecting on her own loss then continued:

"How is your grandfather, I really enjoyed talking to him when we met at the charity match."

"Grandpa is very well! His arthritis is a bit bothersome at times, but he's very spritely for his 70s."

"He is very fond of you, isn't he?" Libby said affectionately. "I remember him being quite protective of you when we were watching cricket all those years ago at the charity cricket match."

"Really, in what way?" I couldn't think what conversation would make her think he was protective.

"I'm not too sure now to be honest, it's a very vague memory, now but he did say it was *your story to tell* and that one day you may get to know me well enough to tell me about it. I remember we were having an interesting discussion about nicknames at the time because it brought back a memory of when I first met you at a bus stop in fact! At the time I didn't realise that we were talking about you, of course. It was a very surreal moment when you turned up at the end of the match!"

As Libby had been talking, I thought back to the day of the charity match. There was an incident on the cricket pitch when my old nickname had been used. That must have been what had triggered the conversation between them about nicknames. Grandpa always hated the use of nicknames, saying that they were invariably given by the powerful to people with less power and often used for derision and control.

I looked at Libby, she was so open and genuine. There was nothing in her that would let me believe she could be anything but kind-hearted. I took her hand that lay on the table and held her gaze. She looked a little startled, so I smiled and explained: "Grandpa was right, there is a story to tell, it starts with a nickname, it's a long story and not a good one. I will tell you my story, but not today when we only have a short time. Is that OK with you?"

Libby placed her hand on top of mine and said: "It's your story to tell or to keep as you wish, I will listen, if and when you are ready to tell it, but for now, let's just enjoy this afternoon, agreed?"

"Agreed."

After our leisurely coffee and sugary indulgences, we ambled around the various shops. Through the glass roof of the Great Western Arcade, we could see that the sun was shining.

"Shall we explore a little bit of the area before you have to head off?" Libby suggested.

We came out of the arcade and onto Temple Row, just a short walk to Cathedral Square where we had a quick stroll around St Phillips Cathedral then made our way to Colmore Row. Libby pointed to a large building a few yards away.

"That's the Royal Bank of Scotland, it's where I'll be starting work on Monday. Isn't it a beautiful building?"

We walked down to have a closer look at the building then continued onto Chamberlain Square where we saw the art gallery that Libby seemed very interested in.

"I think they have a big pre-Raphaelite collection in this art gallery," she said as we walked towards the steps. "I'd like to see that one day, but we don't have time to do it justice today!"

I was very impressed; I hadn't realised she was an art enthusiast. She looked a little disappointed, and I wondered if there was a gallery shop we could look at instead.

"Let's see if there is a shop." I suggested, "We might be able to buy some postcards or posters?" In the end, we managed to buy a poster of Rossetti's *Proserpine* for Libby's new flat. She said the picture reminded her of her friend Jenny because of the girl's long red hair, but also because it was Jenny that introduced her to the pre-Raphaelites.

We strolled back to the cathedral and sat in the sunshine on one of the benches.

"The temperature is definitely a few degrees warmer down here than in Edinburgh," Libby said, taking off her jumper and tying it around her neck. The sight of her lemon jumper brought back another memory – the day of the Bowie concert and the *mystery of the incredible shrinking jumper.* As I glanced at her jumper I saw her bristle for a second. I smiled at her then she relaxed. A sudden recollection made her jump, and she playfully punched my shoulder:

"Don't you dare mention my jumper," she threw her head back and laughed at the memory. "God that was so embarrassing with everybody staring at me!"

She sat back on the bench, soaking up the sunshine, her eyes closed.

"Mmmm, this is nice!"

I smiled, and let my arm drop around her shoulders, she looked up at my face then rested her head on my shoulder. She was quiet for a while, then in a broad Fife accent that I'd never heard her use before, she said sternly:

"Ye ken, ah'm a respectable wee lass frae Cupar and ah've always bin taught nae tae make th' the first move," then back to her softer Scottish lilt she continued "but I really hope that you get that job and move down to Birmingham and if you do, I really hope that we manage to see each other again. I've got a good feeling about you Dr Ashford."

I kissed her forehead, "Whatever happens, I'm going to make sure that we see each other again! In fact," I search my pockets and overnight bag for a pen and some paper and started scribbling some numbers, "this is the number to get hold of me at Grandpa's. There will always be somebody to answer the phone and they will always pass on a message. This is the number of the hospital I am currently working at, but it could be difficult to get hold of me. And this is my current home number. Although I'm not likely to be living there for too much longer. Let me take your number too and then it won't just be you having to do all the chasing."

Libby looked at my scribbles and back at me, "Can I just double check that what I think this says is what you have actually written – you doctors have notoriously bad handwriting you know! I've been in this position before and ended up with the wrong number!"

Having exchanged numbers and agreed that they were all correct, we sat back and enjoyed the late afternoon sun. We could hear the noise of starlings and see them coming to nest on the roofs of the high Victorian buildings. I had a fleeting thought that this was early for starlings, but I was enjoying the sound and sight, and even more, enjoying Libby's company. She turned to me and said quietly: "This last year was a bit of a difficult one for me, but I think this is a turning point. You know our paths have crossed so many times but for one reason or another, it never seemed to be the right time for us to be together. Perhaps this is the right time now?"

"I think it is," I said, her face so close to mine, her eyes so sparkling. I bent closer and kissed her deeply, wrapping my arms around her as she responded.

Someone walking along the path shouted in a very broad Brummie accent, "*Gerra ruuwwm, yow pehhhr!*" Then laughed as he continued his walk, leaving us bewildered.

We both pulled apart, grinning. "What did he say?" I asked laughing, not quite understanding the accent.

"I think it was something like 'get a room you pair'"

"Oh really?" I said, smiling, wiggling my eyebrows at her hopefully.

"Behave yourself," she slapped my arm playfully "you'll be late for your train."

"Oh God, what time is it?" Looking around, the Saturday afternoon bustle had gone, and everything was much quieter. I looked at my watch. "What? That can't be right! It's 6:45, my train left 15 minutes ago!"

# 11
# Libby – Birmingham, September, 1988

After a frantic rush to New Street Station, and a surprisingly sympathetic discussion between the ticket office and Dr Ashford (I think the Doctor status played a big part in the sympathy vote), Tim managed to exchange his ticket for a train departing at 4 pm tomorrow afternoon. There was no possibility of taking a later train today because the big football team in the city had been playing and the away fans were returning to Manchester, so the train was packed.

That left the problem of where Tim would stay for the night. Tim had gallantly said he would look for a cheap hotel in the area, but at such short notice on a Saturday night he was struggling to find anything at all that wasn't extortionately priced.

I decided to phone Sandra and asked if she would mind if he stayed on the sofa. Her response was outrageously down to earth: "If I had a gorgeous doctor with a problem like that, he'd be in bed with me, not on my sofa!" Taken aback, and at the back of my mind wondering if she ever thought about

AIDS, I said uncertainly, "We're not quite at that stage of our relationship yet."

She gave a deep, hearty, infectious laugh. "Oh well, don't hang about girl! But by the way, have you noticed that the chair in your room is a futon? He might be better off on that than the sofa. Whatever, it's not a problem for me one way or the other, I'm not your Mom."

"Thanks Sandra, that's great, I'll let him know."

I felt quite unsure as to how to approach it with Tim, and in the end, I just blurted it out.

"So, erm, cards on the table Tim. I've just spoken to Sandra, and it turns out that there is a futon chair in my room, so you're welcome to make use of that tonight, or you can use the sofa in the sitting room. But, just so you know, I'm not ready to sleep with you if you get my meaning so, if you're OK with that, then you're welcome to stay."

Tim stared at me for a moment but didn't say anything and I thought that maybe I'd been too blunt, I felt a flush creep up from my chest to my neck to my face.

A huge grin spread across his face.

"I would be honoured to take up your offer, and of course I will be nothing but a gentleman. I would expect nothing less from *'a respectable wee lass from Cupar'* and will be on my best behaviour all times."

I had to chortle at his terrible Scottish accent, but I appreciated his making light of the situation.

"You'll have to work on your Scottish accent it you want to take the Mick out of me! That was terrible!"

As we came down the ramp from the Pallasades Shopping Centre, above the station, we passed a McDonalds so grabbed a bite to eat then following Sandra's instructions we navigated our way back to Selly Park on the bus route. It was odd seeing blue and cream buses turn up rather than the familiar maroon and white of the Edinburgh buses, something else I was to get used to.

❖❖❖

By the time we got back to the flat and got everything organised with spare pillows and blankets, it was almost ten o'clock at night so while Tim was in the sitting room, I got ready for bed.

"I'll leave you to watch the end of the news if that's OK with you? By that time the bathroom will be free, and I'll be decent, so you should be safe to come into the room."

Tim was as good as his word, and very discreet and gentlemanly. With the lights out, talking seemed to come even more easily to us and we carried on talking well into the early hours of the morning.

I had wondered why he mentioned his grandparents so much but never his parents and was deeply shocked to find out that his parents had been killed in a car accident not long before he started university.

"I was 17 at the time and had just finished my mock A'Levels." Tim explained. "I always spent the holidays with my grandparents because Mama and Father were always travelling. To be honest, I wasn't very close to them at all. Father was very distant from me, he was very severe, with a stiff upper lip, didn't like to see boys snivelling or being weak."

"You mean the sort of man who would say 'big boys don't cry?'" I asked, there was a pause before Tim answered, then he cleared his throat and continued.

"He was a difficult man to like. Mama was very beautiful, but I don't think she was particularly maternal. Once they had their 'son and heir' there was no possibility of another pregnancy as far as she was concerned."

"Grandpa was more of a father to me, and Grandma when she was around was of course just like a mother. When she died, I was only ten years old, I was inconsolable. So, when my parents were both killed and I was only 17, I felt like I had no more grief to give. It was like losing distant relatives, not my own parents. I know that makes me sound like a terrible person, but they just weren't present in my life."

"Gosh, you look at people and think how *together* and *well balanced* they are. You have your own picture in your head about their life and their past and you can't imagine what they could have gone through. I don't think what you told me makes you sound like a terrible person at all, but I am so sorry that you have had to deal with all that at such a young age. You do seem very well balanced to me, despite it all!"

"Libby, you are a very sweet girl, and I'm sorry to say that you don't know the half of it. I still have a story to tell, and one day when I do, you may not find me so well balanced."

I couldn't imagine what more this poor, kind man could have gone through, but I did not want him to suffer this alone. I trusted him and I wanted him to trust me. Sliding out of my bed, I slid under the covers next to him and put my arms around him as he slid his arm under my shoulders.

"If it is such a terrible story, you should have someone to comfort you while you're telling it. If you are ready to share your story, I am happy listen, but I won't be judging how balanced you are, I'll just be here to listen."

And so, Tim disclosed his long-guarded boyhood secret story, starting from the day the nickname was given, up to the day of the abuse. All the while I cradled him and soothed him while he talked about how the school responded; how his grandpa supported him; and how his father responded. He disclosed the flashbacks that he still had, the impact that these had on his life, how he had been reluctant to date girls because of his feelings of inadequacy. The trauma and the impact of this went on, we talked on and on through the night and into the morning, just holding on to each other. It had been a cathartic experience for both of us and we were drained but paradoxically replete. The extreme emotions that we had explored had opened up a reservoir of warmth, affection and intimacy that would help in the healing processes to come.

❖ ❖ ❖

# Part 3

# 12
# Libby – Sandstone Manor, December, 1990

I really didn't know what to expect from Tim's family home. He called it Sandstone Manor, but I hadn't expected it to actually be a Manor House of this size. The long sweeping drive looped around a pristine, manicured circular lawn leading to the elegant Georgian pink sandstone building. The central building, with its magnificent columns and steps was balanced beautifully by the symmetrical side buildings of the stables and kitchens.

Two years ago, on my first visit to Sandstone Manor, I remember walking into the vast, pale yellow entrance hall with its beautiful decorative ceiling. I had the sensation of being gazed upon by cherubs looking down at me from the enormous medallions that were carved into the ceiling and despite the overwhelming grandeur, a sense of tranquillity washed over me.

I remember that first visit, arriving at Sandstone Manor, as I sat in the pale duck-egg blue Georgian drawing room, and I felt that we were worlds apart. I looked at the baby grand piano in the corner, shaded by the heavy drapes; at the silk accent chairs; at the original art collection and I felt that I could never belong in this world. As I waited apprehensively for someone to greet me, I glanced at some family photographs. There were some younger pictures of Phillip with what must have been his wife and daughter. Phillip was debonair and dashing in his pictures and his wife was very beautiful, as was the little girl alongside them. Glancing at a later photograph of their daughter as a bride, I could see that she did indeed turn into a very beautiful woman as Tim had described. There were of course many pictures of Tim and his grandpa: Tim in cricket whites; Tim on walks; on a bike; fishing; graduating. Many of them with his grandpa's arm protectively around his shoulders. I remember that day, sitting in the drawing room, sighing, thinking again how difficult it would be to belong to a world like this, with staff to cook for you and take your bags to your room.

And then Phillip (or rather Sir Phillip as I had been informed) came in to the drawing room to find me.

"Elizabeth, my dear, how lovely to see you again. Or should I say Libby?" Phillip kissed my cheek and put his arm round me in a warm, paternal way.

"I'm sorry that you've been left on your own, and in this stuffy room too! We rarely use it to be honest, far too formal for us. Why don't we take ourselves to the snug where it's more comfortable? Tim has just telephoned, and he will be with us this afternoon. I can't tell you how pleased I am that you and young Tim have started dating. It fills my heart you know!" It took no time at all for us to start chatting away like we had when I first met him all those years ago. He was so welcoming, and I was beginning to believe that perhaps I could belong here after all.

❖❖❖

Tim and I have been 'dating' as Phillip so quaintly put it for over two years now. I have been strictly forbidden to refer to Tim's grandfather as Sir Phillip, and Grandpa doesn't sit easily with me either, so we have agreed that *Phillip* will be fine for now.

Tim and I have travelled up separately on this occasion. It means that we can have both cars with us because we are due to spend a couple of days here at Sandstone, then I will travel on to Cupar to stay with Dad for Christmas, so it won't leave Tim without a car when he has to dash off back for work.

I seem to have been left to my own devices, however, because Phillip is in his study having an aperitif with an old friend and bemoaning the performance yet again of the England cricket team in the current Ashes Test Series. Apparently, England lost their first encounter in Brisbane by ten wickets, so the boxing day test match in Sydney is a must win as far as Phillip is concerned!

I smile to myself as I think of his passion for the game.

Tim should be arriving any time now, so I finish unpacking my case, carefully removing the Christmas gifts I brought for everyone, making sure that they still had their bows and tags in place. I hear noises coming from the vast echoey hall so make my way downstairs. I am astounded to not only see Tim but my dad standing in the entrance hall and stop dead in my tracks.

"Dad! What are you doing here? I…? Tim?"

I gave up and ran firstly to my dad throwing my arms around him, then giving Tim the same treatment, but looking questioningly from Dad to Tim and to Phillip who had just come out of the study with his friend.

"Look who I found on the way from Birmingham!" Tim said.

I gave him a questioning look, expecting to be told what was going on, but he said nothing. It was Phillip who came to my rescue: "Libby, I hope you don't mind, but I'm afraid we've rather scuppered everybody's plans for Christmas! We wanted to have a bigger family Christmas this year, so we have coerced your father into joining us."

Dad continued the explanation. "So, change of plan Libby, I decided to take up Phillip's offer and come here for Christmas, so we can all spend more time together and do less travelling."

"Well, that's great, but why all the subterfuge? Why didn't you just tell me then we could have travelled up together?" I said, still a little mystified.

"I can answer that," Dad said, "you see, Tim needed to have a wee chat with me about something very important, so he came up to Cupar and gave me a lift back here." He nodded his head towards something behind me and I turned around expecting to face Tim. But when I turned, instead of being face-to-face with Tim, I found him on one knee with a ring in his hand. My heart fluttered wildly, and my stomach did a summersault.

"Miss Elizabeth Fraser, this was never going to be the most romantic gesture ever, because I'm not very good at that sort of thing, but I have spoken to your dad, and he has no objections to me asking if you would do me the greatest honour of being my wife."

I looked at Tim, the shy, hardworking, compassionate, caring man that I had grown to love, a relationship that was so nearly squandered many years ago when our lives could not seem to keep on the same path or in the same direction. I felt tears prickle behind my eyes and I could see the emotion nearly overwhelming Tim too.

I looked at the ring he was holding, it was a beautiful Art Deco, diamond solitaire ring, I had never seen such a beautiful ring in all my life. It was flanked with six more diamonds, three set in each shoulder with a platinum band. It was absolutely stunning. I was afraid to speak at that moment as Tim held my gaze. It felt as though all the other people in the room had melted away and that we were the only people present. We were lost in each other's gaze but somehow able to communicate everything we needed to in a single, silent, intimate moment. He took my hand, still gazing into my eyes and with the slightest nod of my head, he placed the beautiful ring on my finger.

"This was Grandma's engagement ring," he said, his voice trembling. I looked at Phillip who smiled and nodded at Tim to continue.

"Grandpa bought the ring for Grandma just before the start of the Second World War, it was made in about 1915 so almost considered antique even then. They had wanted Mama to wear it on her wedding day but she thought it was too old fashioned at the time so it was put in to a trust, waiting for someone special. Grandpa gave this ring to me when I told him I wanted to ask you to marry me. That special person is you Libby."

And this time I really did cry.

Tears were running down my cheeks now. I turned to Phillip and embraced him. "Thank you for entrusting me with this beautiful ring, I will take care of this and of Tim."

Then turning back to Tim, I smiled and said, "Dr Timothy Ashford, I would be honoured to be your wife."

Everyone cheered and seemingly from nowhere some champagne and glasses appeared ready for a toast.

Phillip was the first to offer congratulations and again it brought me to tears as he spoke about Tim from his heart.

"You all know how dear to me young Timothy is," he said, clasping an arm around Tim's shoulder. "Having lost my wife and daughter many years ago, Tim became the raison d'etre in my life, Tim is not just my grandson, but my friend and confidant. But with only Tim and myself left in the family, I can't tell you how delighted I am that Libby has agreed to marry Tim and that she and her father, Mr Fraser will be part of the family. Here's to Tim and Libby and to families."

Everyone cheered again and I walked over to Dad and hugged him. "That was nice of Phillip to include me in the toast," Dad said. "And it was good of Tim to talk to me first and ask my permission," he continued, smiling as he watched his future son-in-law shaking hands with everyone, "but I would always expect you to be your own woman, you know that don't you?"

I smiled and hugged him again as he continued "This was the same laddie that you spoke about all those years ago with your mum, wasn't it? She would have loved to see you here now, so happy. I liked that laddie from the first time I met him, but there was a sadness about him I couldn't quite fathom. I think there's been a lot of healing in the past few years and that must be down to you. I think you're very good for each other Libby."

"I think so too Dad," I said as I gazed at my new fiancé and we exchanged smiles from across the room.

It was a wonderful start to Christmas and the celebrations went well into the new year. It was delightful for Dad to be surrounded by lots of people and feel part of a family and by the time we were ready to return to Cupar, he already had a firm commitment to return to the Manor for a visit in the spring.

❖❖❖

# 13
# Libby – Birmingham, September, 1998

I arrived at work early this morning and the department is eerily quiet. Today has been exactly ten years since I moved down to Birmingham so I indulge myself and take some time to reflect on everything that has happened in those intervening years.

Bumping into Tim on the train was the catalyst of many things that happened. Of course, my life would never have been what it is now without that – imagine if we had taken different trains? Where would my life be if we hadn't been on that train at that time?

Within three years of that meeting we were married, not even three years in fact. It was two months short of three years, July 1991. What a beautiful day we had. It was a small simple wedding, neither of us wanted anything extravagant so just our best friends: my friend Jenny and her partner Hugo and Tim's old friend James from his school days and his partner as guests along with Dad and Grandpa. There was a beautiful reception at Sandstone Manor, it was all we could have wished for.

I feel like I have been really blessed. As a wedding present Phillip gave us an enormous lump sum from the family trust fund to purchase our house in Moseley. It needed some work, but I've loved working on it. It's a beautiful four-bedroomed Victorian house, still with some original features like the fireplaces, intricate coving and ceiling roses, floor tiles and stained glass windows. We fell in love with it and were able to buy it outright without a mortgage thanks to the trust fund. It was in a perfect position both for Tim's work and easy for me to get into town to the bank. Of course, I thought by now we would have filled the house with more children, but that was not to be. We have our beautiful little boy, Josh who we were blessed with but it seems that no medical intervention will bless us with another child. I think that as we were both only children ourselves, it hasn't really phased us if we're honest, but part of me still wishes for a little brother or sister for Josh.

I think back to the day Josh was born in April 1993. It was such a long, drawn-out labour but the moment that he was handed to me, and I looked down at his little face and he clenched my finger with his tiny fist, I felt that I had known him all my life. There were so many features that were familiar to me, that reminded me of my family. I finally understood what my mum must have felt, and realised that you really don't know how much your own mum loves you until you have a child of your own.

I look at the pictures on my desk. There is a plethora of pictures of Josh, from his birth up to the five-year-old that he is now. As I look at the pictures, I can see that he has grown a little more like Tim's side of the family now. I recollect a picture of Tim's mother that always sat on the piano in the drawing room at Sandstone and I can see a resemblance in Josh, particularly in his eyes, to that picture. I pick up one of the pictures and look at it closely, it's a snap of us as a family, taken in Scotland and I sit back for a moment to reminisce about the holiday.

As much as we like living here in Birmingham, Scotland seems to be our *happy place*. We always take our holidays in Scotland, primarily because we want to visit the family so whenever we have a break, it's always in Scotland. We do venture further north though and spend some time walking in the Highlands. Josh seems to enjoy scrambling up the smaller hills and is quite the little mountain goat. Tim enjoys more rigorous walks so we usually find trails and recognised paths that have a variety of routes for a range of abilities and leave Tim to enjoy his longer hikes while we enjoy a hot drink and reading time in a cafe.

I love spending time with Josh, but I made the decision that I still wanted to come back to work, part time at least. Then when Josh started school, I increased my hours and whilst I have to be incredibly organised, I can make it work for everybody. It means that I work twice as hard during the day and barely have time to pass the time of day with anybody so that I can get my work done. Behind my back I've heard people call me a number of names like *Ice Queen* or *Frigid Bitch* but I can live with that if it means that I can leave on time and get back to Josh so we can have a meal together, give him his bath and read him a bedtime story.

Today is one of the very rare days that I didn't have to organise getting Josh to the child minder before school because Tim had a day off and wanted to take him to school himself.

I'm still at manager's assistant level, but with my banking exams complete, I'll be looking to move to assistant manager and then manager in corporate banking very quickly. It's such a male dominated world though so I need to be on top of my game and fight my corner. I had a run-in with one of my contemporaries just a couple of months ago when the school rang me because Josh wasn't very well and I had to pick him up. My colleague asked why Josh's dad couldn't pick him up. My response was to ask him how he would feel if he had a brain tumour and the doctor who was operating said, *'sorry I've got to go, but don't worry my bank manager will take over from me.'* Anyway, I informed him, I was able to work from home, I had dial-up network and was contactable by phone and email, whereas a surgeon couldn't work remotely. At least, this job wasn't a life-or-death situation; leaving someone at the operating table would be.

As I say, you really have to fight your corner hard in this industry.

Well, it's not often I get any time to myself in this office and already I can hear some noise in the outer office so I make a start to prepare myself for the day ahead.

❖❖❖

# 14
# Tim – Birmingham, September, 1998

I always think of this day as being the turning point in my life, today is the 10$^{th}$ anniversary of that special train journey when I bumped into Libby. Everything that happened since then has been down to that one single, incredibly fortuitous meeting. We missed out on our wedding anniversary this year because I was in surgery so I thought I would make up for it today and cook her favourite meal tonight. I have the day off and am starting it with breakfast with my amazing boy Josh.

I look at Josh and my heart melts. I think back to my own childhood when my father was so absent and I cannot imagine being absent from Josh's life. My mind wanders further and I think of being sent to prep school then boarding school and my pulse races. I could never send my little Joshy to a school like that.

I remember the day Josh was born. It was such a difficult day for Libby, but she was so stoic and fought through the pain and then after what seemed like an age, our little boy finally arrived. I looked at Josh and at Libby that day and I thought my heart would burst with emotion, I was the luckiest man alive. I never imagined I would be the type of man who could spend hours just staring at a little baby, watching him sleeping, looking at his pink cheeks, his long eyelashes, his arms above his head with his little fists clenched in peaceful abandon. I was mesmerised by this little human being.

The first time Josh said '*Da Da*' was just amazing. There was no way that I was going to have him call me '*Father,*' I was very definite about being called Dad or Daddy.

I look at one of Josh's drawings on the fridge, it's a picture of four stick figures of a time when we were last at Sandstone. Each figure has a label above the head, showing '*Mummy*', '*Daddy*', '*Joshy*' and '*Grampy*'. When Josh was tiny, he thought everybody's name ended with a 'y' so that's what he called Grandpa. Even Libby has started using the name Grampy which he finds very endearing.

Libby is an amazing mum; she works so hard to fit everything in. She has this crazy idea that she has to be everything: the mum, the career woman, the homemaker, the decorator, the baker, the chef. I worry that she will burn herself out, but she tells me that she has everything in hand, she says women *can* have it all these days and it's just a case of being organised. God knows where she gets all the energy from.

Walking Josh to school reminds me of the times when Grandpa and I used to walk along the coastline in Scotland. He was so patient with me when I was a child and answered all my childish questions. Moseley is a busy traffic area so I hold on tight to Josh as we navigate our way to the local primary school and chat about everything and nothing. It's a non-uniform day today and Josh is wearing his favourite Spiderman outfit.

Arriving at the school, he sees his best friends and they run up to each other admiring each other's outfits. Josh is pretending to catch his friends in a spider's web with an imaginary web shooter from the back of his hand. Seeing Josh in imaginary play with his friends is just delightful and as they walk into the school together, it brings a lump into my throat. During Josh's short life I have questioned my Father's parental decision-making on many occasions, but none more so than when he allowed me to board at prep school from such a young age. When I look at Josh and see the joy and freedom of his childhood and how this compares with my own, where I was at the beck and call of the older boys, I can't help but question his decisions.

Josh turns around just before he disappears through the school doors and shoots an imaginary spider web at me. I feign being trapped in the web and he jumps up and down at his success, then giggles his way through the school doors and out of sight.

I think about his happy little face all day, as I shopped and cooked for our anniversary meal. I felt that this beautiful memory of Josh, so happy and giggling his way into school would stay with me for the rest of my life.

# 15
# Libby – Birmingham, April, 2009

I turned over and looked at the clock: 03:05 am. I couldn't stop thinking about the internal memo that had been circulating. It would be a huge decision for me to take and I couldn't make it by myself but it was something that I needed to work out on my own before I broached it with Tim, but he's been so distant lately it's been hard to talk about anything with him.

The bank is in utter turmoil and has been since the government had to bail it out in October last year. We're still not out of the woods and the rumours are that there will be another government bailout later this year so we will be forced into effective nationalisation because the Government will own most of the bank by then. It's hard to believe that a bank as large and established as RBS could amass losses of over £24 billion – the biggest annual loss ever made in UK corporate banking history, but somehow, we had managed to do this. Among the many failings we made was at the start of the global financial crisis, the amount of capital that RBS had in reserve wasn't enough to reassure our investors that we could absorb the losses, or any potential future losses, so investors lost confidence. We also made loans to too many borrowers who didn't have the necessary credit scores. Decision-making at the top level was risky and we were over-exposing ourselves financially. And operationally there was no protocol for challenging these risky decisions. If the male dominant world of corporate banking found it hard to challenge decision-making, they should ask themselves what it feels like to be a woman in this industry when they are hitting their heads on a glass ceiling!

What a mess. I look at the clock again: 03:47 am.

I have to be honest; the fight has gone out of me. I think of the memo again: *voluntary redundancy*. Maybe I should apply for it. But after all the years of fighting my corner, should I really give up the fight? If I gave up my career now, what would I be, *who* would I be?

I reflect on that for a while. Maybe it was time that I stopped defining myself by my career and started thinking about who I actually was. Why was I so fixated on having a career anyway? Was it a 1980's thing that women could have it all: the career; the family; the house? Do everything, be everything? I thought about some of my friends; they didn't seem to have the need to push themselves in the way that I did. What was the drive that kept me in my career? Did I really want to keep fighting in this male dominated business world? Did I really want to keep to such a rigid timetable at home with everything run like a military operation so that I could do everything that I set out to?

I thought about Joshy. Had he missed out on anything because of my job? I had always wanted everything for him but have I given him everything?

I remember my own childhood and how my mum was always there when I came home from school. Josh doesn't have that and never has – he was usually collected from school by a childminder and was picked up from there.

Waves of guilt start to wash over me as I think of things that I could have done if I hadn't been so intent on building a career. Why was I so intent on building a career anyway? Then I recall my last conversation ever with my mum: "Don't let that young laddie get in the way of a career."

Was that what had spurred me to be a career woman? I think of my lovely mum and the last time I saw her. My eyes start to prickle and pool with tears. Even after all these years, I still feel such sadness and loss. It's not as raw as it was all those years ago, but as I think of the last conversation we had, I realise that I have hung onto those words as a kind of subconscious mantra and have not had the courage to face the true grief that was lurking in the background. The grief that is still within me, unresolved. Instead, I am still holding onto those last words that she gave me.

I turn to face the clock, the tears that had pooled in my eyes trickle down my nose and cheek. 04:38 am. I should try to get some sleep. I try to switch off my emotions and think of something else.

I'm in a dark place emotionally at the moment, guilt and remorse sweep over me again and I feel pain rising from my gut at the very thought of what I've done. I did something really stupid that I will regret for the rest of my life. Perhaps leaving the bank would be a way out of that mess too? I stifle a sob; Tim stirs and I lay still so as not to disturb him further and soon I hear the soft breathing sounds of his sleep. I sigh deeply and say in my mind, "I miss you Mum," and am taken back to the times when I was Josh's age when I would say to her, "Can we talk?" and we would take ourselves to the bathroom for a heart-to-heart. Immediately, I imagine the smell of Imperial Leather soap and feel comforted.

I wonder what Mum would think of me now, the career woman with my own family. Would she be proud of the career woman or would she be proud of the mum, or would she be ashamed of the woman I've become? Tears begin again. I think of how much she has missed in my life, that she never got to meet Tim or her beautiful grandson.

I start to think about Josh. I can't believe my little boy will be 16 in a couple of weeks. My lovely boy, I know there is something bothering him, but I can't seem to get him to talk to me about it. He seems distant somehow and Tim doesn't seem to have that closeness with him that he used to either. They were inseparable when Josh was little, but lately they seem to be drifting. Maybe I'm just not around enough to see what's going on. Perhaps voluntary redundancy would be the right thing for us all right now.

My mind turns to my mum again, if she were here now and I could ask her what I should do, I wonder what she would advise me? I mentally place myself with her in our old bathroom in Cupar and think of how we would discuss the voluntary redundancy. In my mind, we might talk about the difficulties of work, about the guilt I feel about parenting, about my relationship with Tim. I tell her about my concerns with Josh, how quiet he has been lately. I tell her that something is bothering him but that I can't get him to talk about it; that his GCSE's are very near and maybe that's it, so I need to support him more than ever now.

In my mind, I hear my mum's gentle Scottish lilt responding to me, telling me that Josh knows how much I love him. She tells me that I have achieved what I set out to do in terms of my career, that as a female corporate manager it's something to be very proud of. She tells me it's time to think about myself and my family and Dad and to let the bank look after itself. After all, she says, you've given the bank many, many years of your life, now it's time for yourself.

I turn to look at the clock again: 05:27 am, the birds are starting to sing their dawn chorus, and the alarm will be going off in half an hour. But I feel calmer now and think I will talk to Tim about voluntary redundancy. I feel that I'm ready to walk away from my career now, to put the past behind me and forget the mistakes. It's been a rough few months, and I won't be sad to be leaving. There's a lot to think about with Josh and his GCSE exams, then $6^{th}$ form, then university. I close my eyes and finally feel sleep take me over.

# 16
# Tim – Birmingham, April, 2009

Libby had another sleepless night last night. I could hear her tossing and turning and checking the clock. I heard her because I was awake too, trying not to disturb her. I can't tell her what keeps *me* awake at night; I can't even bring *myself* to think about what is keeping me awake at night.

The flashbacks started again when Josh was about 13 and have been getting worse over the last three years. It started one day when I had taken Josh swimming, we had just come out of the pool and Josh and I had gone to the male changing rooms. Josh was drying himself and chattering away about the school play and the main part that he desperately wanted. The school were putting on a performance of *A Midsummer Night's Dream* and Josh was up for the part of Puck.

Being in the changing room with Josh triggered a really vivid and traumatic flashback and I couldn't concentrate on what he was saying. There were some older boys in the bay next to us who had been in the gym, I could smell the acrid adolescent sweat as they stripped off their gym cloths ready for their showers. I was urgently trying to control my breathing and avoid it turning into a panic attack. I just sat still on the bench in our bay and tried to calm myself down. It had come out of the blue, but I was transported back to my own school days and the hideous communal showers. It was the smell that triggered it, that pungent smell of adolescent sweat.

Josh was my son, my beautiful boy, but as I looked at him now, with a sudden realisation, it struck me that he was no longer a little boy, he was an adolescent. He was roughly the same age I was when the abuse happened at boarding school all those years ago. Then an awful thought crossed my mind: how did Josh feel about being in a communal changing room? I had never asked him, what if he felt uncomfortable? Was he comfortable about physical contact with another man, a grown man? I had never talked to him about that either. But I'm his dad, surely it was acceptable for me to have physical contact with him. What if he didn't want me to put my arm around him though? What if he didn't like it but didn't want to tell me that he didn't like it?

At that time, in the changing room with Josh, my breathing had begun to get harder to control, my pulse had started racing and I could feel a cold clamp beginning to constrict the base of my skull. I had tried to relax, taking slow deep breaths.

I tried to imagine putting my arm around Josh's shoulders in the way I always did, but as I imagined this, my pulse started racing even faster. What was wrong with me? This was my son; I was his dad. But every time I thought of putting my arm around him, I felt like a predator, a perpetrator. I couldn't look at Josh, I felt as though this beautiful little boy would be tarnished by my past, I felt that I could no longer hug him in the way that I could when he was a little boy.

My thoughts had been interrupted.

"So, what do you think, do you think I'd make a good Puck?" Josh had said, "Dad, Did you hear me? Are you OK Dad, you haven't even started getting dried?"

I had made some sort of response, took some deep breaths and tried to concentrate on what Josh was saying.

"Sorry. Sorry Josh, I just feel a bit dizzy, my blood sugar must be a bit low, that's all. Just give me a minute and I'll be fine."

I couldn't let him see me break down so gathered myself together and managed to hide my anxieties from him, that time.

That was three years ago now, but since then I haven't been able to shake the feeling of needing to keep my distance from my own son. Every time I think about physical closeness, I have a flashback or start to show the symptoms of a panic attack and then I have to work hard to avoid a full-blown panic attack.

The worst thing about it now is that Josh has withdrawn from me completely. I know that's down to my avoidance of him, but I can't talk to him about it. There's such a void between us now. In the old days, I would have talked to Grandpa about us, but he's very frail now so I don't want to upset him with this. He has enough on his plate at the age of 93.

# 17
# Josh – Birmingham, May, 2009

"Why can't I go to Sandstone? I'm old enough to travel by myself and I'll be good company for Grampy."

I know I sounded like a whiney little boy but it seemed so unfair that I wasn't allowed to go. I had study leave for my GCSE's coming up and it seemed like a great place to study for the exams. I could go up for the half term holiday and get some work done and maybe stay a bit longer if Grampy was up to it. It felt like everyone was walking on eggshells in this house and I was finding it difficult to concentrate. I thought it was a great idea.

"Josh, Grandpa is 93, and very frail."

I knew Dad would say that, and I knew Gramps was very old, but I also knew that I wouldn't get in his way or wear him out so I persisted with my arguments until eventually Dad gave in. I also thought that he would be able to persuade Mum, but Mum had her own bombshell to tell us. It turned out that she had been made redundant from the bank and wouldn't be working any more. She had been given *gardening leave* too so she was leaving the bank immediately so that she couldn't take any state secrets from the bank or poach customers away or something like that, but it actually meant that she was getting paid for doing nothing. Nice one, Mum!

In the end, it was decided that Mum would drive me up to Sandstone then would carry on to Grandad's in Cupar.

❖❖❖

It was really cool at Sandstone Manor, there was always so much to see and lots of walks to do. Grampy wasn't able to walk much now, but he was such a cool dude. He had so many stories to tell about when he was younger. I was careful to make sure that I didn't wear him out, but he seemed happy to speak to me about his past so whenever he was willing, I was ready to hear about it. It was really cool that he had served in World War II because this was one of the subjects for my GCSE history so it was like revision too.

I loved looking at the photograph albums from the old days and Grampy could remember pretty much everything about all the people. He knew some really famous people from those days too, including film stars and politicians. They were all really handsome and so well dressed, not like the celebrities you see on TV today with their scruffy hair and torn jeans. These stars had crisp white shirts and bow ties and dinner jackets. Even if they were casually dressed, they still wore a suit. The men were very attractive and so well groomed.

"It's funny that we don't have any photographs of Dad's family at home," I said one day. "I don't remember ever seeing any photographs of Dad's parents. I don't even think I know what they looked like."

"Well, my boy," Grampy started – this usually meant that he was about to embark on a long story, so I was intrigued to find out what this might be.

"Your dad had a very difficult childhood; he lost his parents in a car crash when he wasn't much older than you. It was a lot for him to take in at such a young age. And of course, his father was absent for much of his life due to his work, it took him abroad for many months at a time. That was why Tim went to boarding school. He wasn't very happy at school either so all in all, it was a very difficult time for him. When his parents died, I think he just shut everything out to stop the pain. That's why he doesn't talk about them or have any pictures of them in the house. It's as though it would remind him of a time in his life when he was very unhappy."

"That doesn't sound like a very healthy thing for anybody to do, I'm sure I would want to talk about it if anything happened to Mum and Dad."

"Yes, I'm sure you would Josh, but everyone has their own way of dealing with grief, I just hope that he has worked it out now and that the grief has been resolved."

"Do you have any photos of him with his parents? Or any photos of his parents at all? I'd like to see them if you wouldn't mind?"

"Yes, there are a few. I tell you what, I'll leave you to get on with some work and I'll have a scout around." Grampy looked wistful. "You do remind me of your grandmother, Eleanor, you know, she was very beautiful; she was our only child. After she died, there was only your dad until Libby, your mum, came along, and then you, of course."

I'd never heard Grampy talk like this before, he sounded so sad. As I looked at him, I saw such affection on his face that I walked over to him and gave him a big hug and he squeezed me back, holding me for a while.

"Aww, Gramps, I feel all choked up, I haven't had a hug like that in ages. I needed that!"

"Any time my boy," Gramps said patting me on the shoulder and he left me in search of the photograph albums.

Left alone, I was distracted by the thought of Grampy's hug. Why did it feel so unusual? I thought back to the last time Dad and I had hugged like that and I actually couldn't remember any physical contact with Dad for months, maybe years. Physical contact felt like such a human need, why had we just stopped hugging? I should talk to him about it when I get home.

❖❖❖

Later that day, Grampy had unearthed a pile of photograph albums and we sat in the snug pouring over them. There were lots of photos of my grandmother Eleanor and even I could see that she really was very pretty. The fashion going from the 1950s to the 1960s and 1970s was crazy but she was still very elegant with it. She was fashionable but understated and graceful.

I could see what Grampy meant about me looking like my grandmother. In the later colour photos, even though they were a bit faded, I could see that we had the same hair colouring and the same nose and eye shape and high cheekbones.

My grandfather, Edward looked like he had a hard side to him, I could feel that unpleasant quality lurking through the photographs. He was definitely not the sort of person you would want to cross. He was a very handsome man but there was a self-assurance about him that could be mistaken for arrogance or even narcissism (my new favourite word!) I looked at the photographs of Eleanor and Edward together and I felt quite sorry for my grandmother. It was as though her presence was being overshadowed by his dominating character.

As we browsed through the many photograph albums, I pointed out a couple of the famous people that I recognised.

"Don't you think the men were better groomed in the old days Grampy? Look, all the men are wearing trilby hats during the day, and top hats and tails in the evening. It was such a glamorous time. Not like today, we haven't got clothes anything like that!"

Grampy chuckled, "So tell me, is there a girl whose eye that you particularly want to catch with a top hat and tails?"

I paused, and we made eye contact for a little too long to be comfortable. I looked away then said awkwardly, "No, there's no particular girl at all."

Grampy said nothing but nodded. He had this way of saying nothing that made you want to tell him everything.

I made eye contact with him again.

"I'm not actually sure I like girls to be honest. I think I like boys more."

I desperately wanted him to say something, but again he just nodded.

Then after a while he said, "It seems like this has been on your mind for a while. Is it something that you want to talk about more?"

I swallowed a lump in my throat, I wasn't sure I wanted to take this any further, but I'd started the conversation so I couldn't clam up now.

"I've never told anybody about this, I wasn't even sure myself if I did like boys. But now that I've said it out loud, I think I do like boys better than girls. If I think of girls, I guess they can look nice, but I don't feel like I want to kiss them or anything. The boys at school are all talking about snogging and having sex with girls already. I just can't imagine myself being with a girl at all."

"I see, and when you see an attractive boy, can you imagine yourself being with him?" Grampy always seemed to be so direct with his questions, there was nowhere to hide when you had a conversation with him.

"Well, sometimes yes. Not always though. There are some boys that I think I'd like to be with but not all of them."

Grampy smiled. "Well, I imagine that would be the same if you were interested in girls, you wouldn't want to be with every girl, but there would be some that you were attracted to, and some that you wouldn't find attractive at all. That applies to boys too."

Having this conversation with Grampy felt like a weight had been lifted from me. He didn't make me feel like a freak and he wasn't acting like he was repulsed; it was such a relief to finally talk to someone about it.

"So, Josh, if you haven't been sure yourself about whether or not you like boys more than girls, am I to assume that you haven't approached any boys or talked to another boy about being attracted to them?"

"No way, I wouldn't know where to start! What if I misread the signals and they called me out and told everybody at school that I fancied boys? I would never live it down!"

"I see, I'm sorry to ask this Josh, but do you feel an element of embarrassment about your feelings for boys? I'm just trying to understand where you are at the moment, I'm not trying to make you feel uncomfortable."

Again, the direct questions. What was Grampy like? It was a good point though. Yes, I did feel some embarrassment about my feelings because I was different from the other boys, everyone else either had a girlfriend or was trying to get into some girl's knickers. I didn't feel part of their world, I was an outsider so yes, I did feel an element of embarrassment and even shame. I tried to explain this to Grampy, and somehow, he knew exactly what I was feeling.

"When your dad was a bit younger than you are now, he was bullied at school, something else from his childhood that he had to deal with. I remember having a conversation with him about feeling insecure because of the bullies. I want you to listen to what I am saying. I don't want you to feel insecure because of your attraction to boys. If people try to belittle you because of it, you mustn't feel devalued, or ashamed. You have a right to be in love with whomever you choose. People should not be persecuted for their beliefs or values or colour or region or sexual orientation. History has taught us that terrible things can happen when people are persecuted for their beliefs and values."

I looked at Gramps with a lump in my throat. At 93 years old, he was still a powerful man, someone who you paid attention to and made you sit up and listen. I was totally in awe of him. "Thanks Gramps, that means a lot."

"Now I take it you haven't spoken to your parents about this yet?"

"No, you're the first person I've spoken to. I know I should talk to them but I didn't know how to even start the conversation."

"Well, when you do speak to your dad, you should tread very carefully and be very gentle with him. I have told you that he had a terrible time at school, he was bullied dreadfully. He has had a great deal to contend with and had many demons to fight over the years. He is not homophobic in any way, but he may have some difficulties of his own to process when you disclose this to him, so please choose your words carefully and be clear in your own mind before you talk to him."

"I don't understand, what difficulties will he have to process?"

"I think that's for your dad to tell you when he is ready but please bear this in mind."

I thought that was a strange thing for Grampy to say. I kept mulling over the phrases he used: *'he has had many demons to fight over the years, he may have some difficulties of his own to process.'* Was Dad gay? That can't be it, he and Mum have a great relationship.

I think back to my earlier thoughts today. Dad definitely hasn't been giving me any physical contact recently, I'm sure it's been years since he actually gave me a hug. There seems to be a distance growing between us. I've been so preoccupied with my own issues that I didn't really notice, but I wonder now if this has anything to do with the demons that he has been fighting. Has he picked up that I'm not interested in girls? Do I give off an aura of being attracted to boys? Could this be the reason that he has distanced himself from me? I don't think I'm ready to talk to my Dad right now. I think it's something that I might keep to myself for a while.

# 18
# Josh – Manchester, September, 2011

When I think of my perfect man, he would probably look like one of the celebs in Grampy's photo album. Definitely someone from the old days, maybe someone like a young James Fox or a young JFK. Someone who was very handsome of course but with a bit of sophistication. Not like the *great unwashed* who populate Manchester University in their grunge, that's for sure! Not one crisp, white shirt among them! Well, maybe I'm being a bit brutal, it *is* only freshers' week after all!

It feels a lot less tense now that I'm away from home. Dad is still his same distant self. I don't know how to approach him – I still haven't been able to talk to him and I couldn't imagine being able come out to him either. I know Grampy wanted me to *tread carefully* but when Dad barely speaks to me it's very difficult to even broach the subject. Things are just so stressy at home, it's been a difficult couple of years. Dad's been working long hours at the hospital and has been like a bear with a sore head when he's at home.

Poor Mum, she was in bits when she left me here in Manchester. She had tears in her eyes for most of the journey up here and she told me that she cried all the way home. She hasn't gone back to any sort of job either so I don't know how she's going to cope being at home all day on her own.

But here in Manchester, I feel like I'm free to finally be me. No more pretending, or hiding who I am. Although I haven't made many friends yet, I still feel very wary of approaching people. The students in my flat are generally nice people though, there's a very sweet girl, Megan who I've made friends with, she clocked straight away that I was gay, which was intriguing: I must be giving off stronger vibes than I thought – either that or she's got a very strong *gaydar* in place. It's great to be able to talk to a girl without them thinking that you're trying it on with them and I think she feels the same with me. She has a great sense of humour and we laugh all the time. I'm sure the other students think we're a couple.

I can imagine Mum having visions of Megan traipsing down the aisle in a white dress with me waiting for her at the altar! I'm going to have to have *the conversation* with Mum sometime soon but how do you tell your mum that you're gay when she's looking forward to a daughter-in-law and grandchildren? I have a few years' grace yet, I don't think even Mum would expect me to be choosing a wife at the age of 18, but I do need to have 'that' conversation soon.

The student accommodation that I'm staying in is pretty good. In my residence, there are blocks of eight flats with eight study bedrooms to each flat. The rooms aren't huge but there's a good-sized desk, chest of drawers, wardrobe, shelving and as a bonus they have an ensuite so at least there's privacy. The kitchen is roomy so it's a good place to socialise, and it seems fairly well equipped for my limited repertoire of dishes. Although, I may well be making use of the pizza takeaway and kebab shops that are only five minutes' walk away!

❖ ❖ ❖

"What about the one in the blue jumper?"

It was lunchtime and Megan was going through all the men in the bar using her spectacularly reliable gaydar, trying to fix me up with a date for a party.

"Not stylish enough," I replied.

"God, you're so picky Josh, no wonder you've never had a boyfriend before!"

"I know, I'm sorry! It's a big thing for me though, I don't just want to jump into bed with anyone!"

"Nobody is asking you to jump into bed with anyone! It's just a party."

"I know that too, but it opens me up to a commitment that I don't know if I can get myself out of. I've never dated anyone before. How do you just say *'thanks but no thanks'* when you've had a date then never want to see them again? I need to at least think that I want to see that person again before I agree to a date."

"OK, I understand. I'll keep looking, but it's your round!" She pointed to the bar and sent me off to get the drinks.

There was a queue at the bar and I found myself standing next to a very handsome man who smelled divine and ironically was actually wearing a very crisp white shirt. Just my type I thought, but where was Megan with her gaydar when I needed her?

I turned to smile at Megan and catch her eye but she was busy on her mobile.

"Is that your girlfriend?" The guy asked nodding at Megan, "She's a pretty girl."

I looked at him, he *was* gorgeous! I smiled at him and looked again at Megan, "No, not my girlfriend, but my very best friend. We're not a couple."

I wondered if I'd been too obvious.

I really wanted to talk to him more, but it was my turn at the bar so I turned to order the drinks. Just as I had paid the barman for the drinks, Megan tapped me on the shoulder and told me that she had to shoot off to drop off her assignment before her next lecture. I looked at the two Pepsi's in my hand: "But I've just bought these, what about your drink?"

"Sorry Josh, I really have to go," then she turned to the guy next to me and said, "Do you fancy a Pepsi mate? It's going free?"

And off she went leaving me standing holding the drinks looking blankly at the guy standing next to me.

"Is she always like that?" he said.

I laughed, "No, but if you fancy a Pepsi, it's going free!"

"Well cheers, Josh is it? I don't mind if I do! I'm Lee by the way."

As we sat down, my mobile vibrated with a message from Megan:

*OMG*
*He perfect 4u*
*Just ur type*
*Spk l8r*

The little sweetie! She had only set me up with this handsome guy! She was adorable, she must have noticed us at the bar and orchestrated the whole thing for me! And amazingly, not only was he handsome, but he was also really easy to talk to. He was doing a BA in English Literature and Creative Writing so we were in the same faculty although on different courses, with mine being modern history and Economics.

We had been chatting for half an hour or so and exchanging information about each other, when Lee said, "So, if Megan isn't your girlfriend, and you're not a couple…?" He left the question hanging with a raise of his eyebrows before continuing, "Would that leave room for me to ask you out for a date?"

It was as simple as that! No stumbling around, no beating around the bush, just a straightforward question.

I paused for a second and felt myself blush, then looked into his gorgeous blue eyes.

"I'd like that very much Lee, but how did you know?"

"It was the way you were smouldering at the bar! You couldn't take your eyes off me. It was pretty obvious!"

"God, that's embarrassing, I'm really sorry, I had no idea!"

Lee laughed gently, "You're new to this, aren't you?"

I didn't want to ruin it before anything even started, but I felt that I needed to be honest with this man right from the start.

"Honestly? I haven't dated anyone in my life! I didn't date girls when I was younger because I felt like a fraud and I didn't know how to approach guys without making a complete idiot of myself. I was quite taken aback when you just asked me for a drink."

Lee laughed again and smiled at me kindly. "So, you're not out of the closet then?"

"Well, my grandpa – I call him Grampy – he knows about me. I told him when I was 16 that I was interested in boys. But nobody else knows. I know I need to have *the conversation* but it's finding the right moment."

"So, you won't be introducing me to your parents just yet then?" Lee said with a wry smile.

❖❖❖

# 19
# Libby – Birmingham, December, 2012

In one way, it feels like an eternity since Josh went to university, but now I can't believe it's coming up for half way through year two already! I'm so looking forward to him coming home for Christmas and he's bringing a friend to stay for couple of days too. I haven't heard very much about his friend, other than the fact that he's in the same school as Josh and doing English and creative writing. I was hoping that he would be bringing his friend Megan home that I've heard so much about but she has had to get back to her family so couldn't make it.

It will be so nice to have the house full again. It feels like the home is complete when Josh is here.

❖❖❖

Lee is a very charming young man, he's clean and tidy and a pleasant houseguest. He makes his bed, offers to help with the dishes and is very polite and chatty.

Josh and Lee are off out tonight into town to the clubs so I expect they will be home very late.

Tim is working late so I'm on my own again.

I'm just taking myself off to bed when the doorbell rings. It's only 11:30 so it can't be the boys; Tim must have forgotten his key, I think as I traipse downstairs again to let him in.

When I get to the front door, I can see two tall, bulky figures through the obscured glass. It can't be Tim or the boys, so I slip the safety chain on and open the door cagily.

"Mrs Ashford?" Two police officers are at the door, showing me their identification – a male and a female officer. I am immediately on my guard, thinking that something terrible must have happened.

"Yes, that's me, I'm Mrs Ashford, is there a problem? Is everything OK?"

"I'm afraid there has been an incident. Two men have been attacked and have been taken to the QE Hospital."

I take a sharp intake of breath as the male officer refers to his notes.

"The victims are Joshua Ashford and Lee Fullertine who I am led to believe is a friend of your son and staying with you?"

"Oh God, yes, Josh is my son and Lee is his friend from university. *Attacked*? Why were they attacked? What happened? They were only going into town to a club. Where were they?"

I was so confused, *victims*? I had so many questions, nothing made any sense. They had only gone into town, I thought they would be safe.

The female officer asked if they could come inside for a minute so that they could explain what had happened, then they would take me to the QE.

The female officer sat me down and explained: "I'm afraid the two men were victims of a homophobic attack. They were on Hurst Street, coming out of The Village Inn in the so-called *Gay Village* part of town."

"What were they doing there? Gay Village? Josh isn't gay! He…? Why was he in the Gay Village? Is Lee gay? What were they doing there? I need to see my son! This is all wrong, there must be a mistake, why was he there in the first place, Josh isn't gay, he would have told me, I'm his mum, he would have told me!"

The officers looked at me patiently, but things started clicking in my brain. Josh had never brought any girls home; he had never shown any interest in girls from school or talked about any girls. The way that Josh and Lee had exchanged glances when they thought I wasn't looking, I had brushed this aside. But I shook myself mentally, thinking that none of that really mattered now. What mattered was that my boy was in hospital and I needed to see him now. I took a deep breath and let it out slowly to calm myself down.

"Please, can you take me to see my son, I need to see him?"

❖❖❖

By the time I got to the ward, both Josh and Lee had been patched up. Fortunately, the injuries were fairly superficial. Cuts and bruises mainly but Josh had taken a blow to the ribs and had two cracked ribs. Tears filled my eyes as I approached him and spilled down my cheeks. They were tears of relief but tinged with sadness that my lovely boy hadn't felt able to talk to me about his sexuality. Did he really feel that it would matter to me that he was gay?

"Mum, I'm sorry! I'm sorry that you had to find out this way. I really wanted to talk to you about it but I just couldn't find a way to tell you." I wrapped my arms around him and tried to cradle him in my arms, then stepped back and looked at him.

"I wish I could hug you like I could when you were a little boy, it's very difficult hugging a six-foot-two young man you know!"

We both laughed, it broke the atmosphere a little.

"I'm sorry too," I said, "I'm sorry that you couldn't talk to me. It makes me feel like I failed as a mother that you couldn't find the right time to tell me! What must you have gone through on your own to get through this?"

"I wasn't entirely on my own. I did tell Grampy, but he said something about Dad having demons of his own and that I needed to tread carefully before I told him so I was just waiting for the right moment."

"I can understand why he would have said that, and that is probably good advice, but I still wish I had known, all that matters for me is for you to be happy, I can't bear to think that you had to deal with this on your own! I think there's a lot of talking and explaining to do – having secrets does nobody any good, but let's get you and Lee back home first."

The doctor was happy to discharge the boys and once the police officers had completed their paperwork and advised Josh and Lee that someone would be in touch with them with any further information they had, they offered us all a lift home.

After several unsuccessful attempts to get hold of Tim on his mobile, we accepted a lift home. We arrived back at the house well after one o'clock in the morning to find that Tim was already at home. He told me that he hadn't been feeling well so had arranged cover for his shift and gone home.

He was sitting on the sofa in darkness in the living room. It was so uncharacteristic of Tim and he already looked on edge, in fact he looked quite fragile, almost traumatised. I was really concerned about him. We had a lot of explaining to do and I wasn't sure he was capable of hearing any of it.

❖ ❖ ❖

# 20
# Tim – Birmingham, December, 2012

Having Lee in the house was creating an intolerable atmosphere. It was hard enough to avoid Josh when he was at home but to avoid Josh and Lee was impossible. I could see the way that Lee looked at Josh and it wasn't healthy. I just wasn't comfortable with Lee being in the house at all.

I needed to protect my family, I had to be there for Josh. I couldn't leave him to someone who might be a predator, someone who might hurt him. I hadn't been in work at all today, I had taken sick leave. I wasn't quite sure what I had intended to do but I found myself driving around all evening to hide the fact that I hadn't been to work from Libby, then eventually I went home to find an empty house.

I was watching them from the darkness of the living room window as they returned home, I felt like an intruder inside my own house. I waited and watched as Libby, Josh and Lee stepped out of the car. I was puzzled as to why they were in a police car; something must have happened, I imagined the worst, and it definitely involved Lee. The security light came on suddenly and illuminated them. I took a sharp intake of breath, it felt like a dagger going straight through my heart. It wasn't just the bruising to Josh's face that sickened me, it was Lee's arm around Josh. I had tried to pretend that everything was OK when Libby came in and found me sitting in darkness, but everything suddenly changed when Josh and Lee followed closely behind. It felt like a vice was holding the back of my neck and my chest, and I couldn't breathe. The last thing I remember was Libby's face then gripping pains in my chest.

❖❖❖

# Part 4

# 21
# Tim – Edinburgh, January, 2013

I was told that the panic attack came on suddenly. I don't remember much about that whole episode if I'm honest. I remember that in my mind, I was picturing Josh as a little boy dressed in his Spiderman outfit, his beautiful little face, beaming with a huge grin and laughing, but then I saw him with all those bruises on his face. The sense of failure that struck me was overwhelming: I had failed him. I had been unable to protect him. I had felt totally crushed.

The suspicions that had been building within me for days, had mingled with feelings from the deep recesses of my mind, feelings, which for so long I had kept out but could no longer suppress. I was terrified and so confused; I remember not being able to breathe; the pain in my chest; the panic and gripping fear; believing I was about die.

Libby had dealt with everything. She has since told me that the paramedics had to administer IV diazepam to control the attack, that everything else had failed to calm me down.

I've been in this private psychiatric clinic in Edinburgh for four weeks now and it has been, and still is an intensive recovery period. Libby had telephoned Grandpa and through his contacts I ended up here. I'm grateful for their sensitivity, there are so many of my colleagues in Birmingham who I could have bumped into if I had been hospitalised there. I know mental illness shouldn't carry a stigma, but I can't face them all knowing about it.

If I'm honest, I knew I needed help and now that I'm in recovery, I can see how badly I needed it. I still have a long way to go and have been signed off sick for another two months at least. When I'm discharged from here, I will stay at Sandstone with Grandpa. Libby will stay with me too so that we can travel up to Edinburgh for my follow-up appointments. It's a blessing that she no longer works, if she had still been working those long hours, I don't know how I would have coped without her.

❖ ❖ ❖

"So how are you feeling today, Tim."

That was a classic opening from any doctor, I thought and resisted the urge to roll my eyes. It was actually the best question that Dr Cuthbert could ask me though, because my feelings had been continually fluctuating.

Dr Cuthbert was the consultant psychiatrist who was assigned to my case and he was extremely able and good at his job. I wouldn't be where I was now if it wasn't for him. I tried my best to answer him as honestly as I could at every consultation, I wanted the recovery to be as quick as possible and I knew that I needed to work with him.

So, when he asked me how I was feeling today, I reflected for a moment and I thought about how I really was feeling: I had been prescribed benzodiazepines for severe anxiety, it was only intended as a short-term treatment and now the dose had been reduced, the anxiety was tolerable so this was a positive step.

"I feel reasonably calm doctor," I replied, "I'm managing my anxiety levels despite reducing the diazepam, the techniques we talked about are helpful, so yes, I'm feeling quite calm."

"That's very good to hear Tim. You are making very good progress."

He looked at his notes for a moment, then looked back at me and said gently: "Now for this session, I want to talk to you about the time when you believe the panic attacks started happening again. I understand there was a period where they virtually disappeared, but when we discussed this last time, you felt that they were triggered again by what you refer to as the c*hanging room episode,* when Josh was about 13 years old, is that correct?"

"Yes, I think it was Dr Cuthbert, I've thought about this a lot. I remember at the time there being a few teenage boys in the changing bay next to us. There are certain smells from my past trauma that can trigger the panic attacks, such as the smell of changing rooms and in particular the smell of boys' sweaty gym clothes."

"I see, and why do you think you then associated the past, traumatic incident with your son?"

"I don't know why it hit me at that point Doctor, but there was a sudden realisation that Josh had reached the same age that I was when I was abused. I remember a feeling came over me and I suddenly felt terrified that I wouldn't be able to protect him like I had been able to protect him up until then.

He became the boy that I was at the point of the trauma, and that boy was incapable of protecting himself I suppose."

"I see," Dr Cuthbert was rapidly making notes, then continued, "that's a useful insight for you to make, I can see that you have been thinking about this period in some detail. Now, tell me, have you come across the term *projection* in your work as a doctor?"

"I recognise the term, but I'm not sure I could give you a definition, I haven't studied psychiatry since my rotation days."

"No, quite, well let me explain it further and relate it to what I think might identify with your situation: Deep in the recesses of our minds we store many thoughts, feelings and memories. Many of these, we would probably prefer not to think about and may even want to deny ever having had. They could be desires or impulses or behaviours towards other people. They may even be fears that we hold on to about how others will behave towards us. These behaviours, in whatever form they are, could be so unpleasant and distasteful to the conscious part of our mind that we need to build a number of defence mechanisms to keep them out. One way of doing this is to project these unpleasant feelings onto other people. By doing this we can actually externalise the problem and push it away from ourselves. This is what we call *projection.*"

"Psychological projection is a defence mechanism that will be instigated when your unconscious feelings start to conflict with your conscious beliefs. In order for you to overcome this conflict, you associate, or assign these feelings to someone else. In other words, you trick yourself into believing that these distasteful qualities actually belong to somewhere else, somewhere that is not a part of you. Are you following me?"

I started to feel very uncomfortable with the way this was going.

"Yes, I think I understand you, so you think that somewhere along the line, in order to cope with these difficult feelings and emotions I have projected them onto someone else rather than admitting to or dealing with the unwanted feelings."

"Precisely, the feelings that you had as a child were swept under the carpet and locked away and as a result, you didn't have the opportunity to resolve the conflict that was within you. The feelings were so painful for you that you needed to ascribe them to someone else."

"This is also why various stimuli such as smells; songs from the past; events such as being in the changing room, were able to trigger such an extreme emotional response. The trigger that occurred when your son was 13 was a critical trigger in many ways. Firstly, it was a memory of a changing room which stirred up traumatic memories."

"Secondly, because Josh was present in the changing room getting changed and was naked, this created an association between the negative traumatic memories and Josh being naked."

"Thirdly, at the time of the trigger, Josh was of a similar age to you when you were abused."

"All of these elements, in your mind created the perfect storm, and the perfect defence mechanism for you to take the feelings that you were not able to deal with as a child and to project them onto Josh."

"If you imagine this whole scenario as an image *physically projected* onto Josh, it will make more sense. With this projected image of yourself imposed onto Josh, in your mind you then looked at him and you could see all the problems that you faced as a child, but instead of them being your problems, you had projected them and made them Josh's problems. In your mind, you see that *he* is in danger of predators, that *you* must protect him, that *he* wouldn't want any man to put his arm around him (even his own father) in case he feels repulsed. These concerns are actually a false concept – they are a projection of your own feelings of course. He doesn't feel these feelings and cannot understand your actions of avoiding him. Are you still following me?"

I feel numb, but I am following Dr Cuthbert. I recall the incident in the changing room very clearly and it was that very episode that appeared to change everything in my life. I could pinpoint the exact moment that the images from my past were projected onto Josh. The analogy of the image being projected onto Josh was very useful because now I could see exactly what happened.

I hesitated before I spoke, but locked eyes with Dr Cuthbert, my eyes filling with sadness and pain, both for Josh and the little boy Tim, who never resolved his traumatic experience.

"Yes, I understand," was all I could say.

Dr Cuthbert gave me a moment to drink some water, then continued.

"I think in order for you to progress over the next few months, there are three main goals for us to look at and I would like you to tell me how you feel about these."

"Firstly, we need to enable you to see your projection for what it is: that it *is* merely a projection and that Josh is not in any danger. If we can enable you to see that the projection is false, then I think you will be able to move forward with your relationship with your son. We can also explore a coping mechanism for you and Josh to come to terms with your relationship and his own sexuality.

"Secondly, we need to enable you to resolve the feelings that you had when you were traumatised. They cannot be resolved if they are locked away, so we do need to relook at these and allow the little boy within you to be healed.

"Thirdly is the issue of your father's response to the trauma. We have discussed this many times, but his response of brushing it under the carpet and not supporting you has, I believe produced a secondary traumatisation for you in that it resulted in you not being able have any contact with him for fear of triggering a panic attack. From what we have discussed, even after your father's death, the thought of his voice or even looking at a photograph of him brought back memories of the event. I think this is going to be the hardest part of the work we do, but I think it will be extremely beneficial.

"There is a lot to work on and I'm sure it sounds quite overwhelming. The one thing that you must remember though is that you had a severe traumatic event in your life, your psychological response to the trauma was a natural defence mechanism and with support, you can unlearn these defence mechanisms. It will take hard work on your part and a lot of soul searching, but if you are in agreement, we can take this one small step at a time and tackle it together."

I felt totally wrung out but strangely euphoric. This session had definitely seen a breakthrough. I was ready to work as hard as it took to rebuild the relationship with my son and agreed wholeheartedly with the goals.

# 22
# Tim – Sandstone, March, 2013

January had turned into February, and then into March. The therapy as predicted had at times been soul searching and hard work. I had reached a point where I could at least look at family photographs. It had been many years since I had looked at these old family albums and I had quite forgotten how beautiful Mama was. Father was foreboding though and still made me want to sit up straight, just by merely looking at his photograph.

Going through therapy helped me realise that I didn't actually grieve for my parents, I just stopped thinking about them and shut away any thoughts of them in a compartment deep within the recesses of my brain. Previously, I wouldn't look at any photographs so that I didn't have to think about my parents, we had no photographs of Mama or Father in our house in Birmingham at all. I was curious to look at them again after all these years.

When they died, I was only 17, but I had been through so much trauma in my short life, including the death of Grandma, that my psyche couldn't deal with any further grief so my mind refused to accept it and just blocked it out completely.

The therapy uncovered more than I had anticipated: as a child I had counted on my father to protect me, but when he dismissed the abuse as just one of those things that happened at school, this became a secondary traumatisation. He had failed me, he should have cared for me and protected me but he just dismissed the whole episode. He would rather uphold the reputation of the school than support me, his only son. It was no wonder that I couldn't look at the photographs, by doing so, it would have opened up a Pandora's box of trauma that little Tim was incapable of dealing with. Little Tim had felt so betrayed by his father that rather than grieve for his father, he locked away his psychological scars so deeply within himself that they were incapable of ever healing.

The therapy was gruelling and traumatic at times, and there were moments when I felt I couldn't continue. Dr Cuthbert always seemed to ask the right questions to get through to me. It was as though he could see into my soul, and of course the prize at the end was always Josh, and rebuilding my relationship with him so however difficult I found it, I never gave in. Libby has been an absolute rock and Grandpa too; I couldn't have managed it without them. I do worry about Grandpa though, he's 97 now and is getting very frail and yet he is still supporting me as he always has done.

Josh is coming to Sandstone for the Easter Break. I haven't seen him since December when I had my '*breakdown*', but we have spoken a few times on the phone. Libby explained to him that I am in therapy for post-traumatic stress disorder – PTSD – I find this phrase rather odd, because I tend to associate it with the military, but I understand that my experiences fall into this category too. If only people had taken it more seriously in 1975, then all of this could have been avoided. There must be so many people of my age and older who have gone through the same traumatic experiences as me and not been supported. Who knows how their lives have been affected as a result?

I have some anxieties about seeing Josh again, but I have built some coping strategies and I am ready to move forward and reconnect with Josh.

❖ ❖ ❖

The days are getting longer and there are the occasional milder, warmer days too now that we are into the end of March. I hear the arrival of a car on the gravel of our driveway and I make my way to the entrance hall feeling apprehensive, knowing that Josh will have arrived. Josh bounds through to the pale-yellow entrance hall, immediately dropping his bag and strides towards me, hesitating for a mere fraction of a second, then throws his arms around me, burying his head on my shoulder. I wrap my arms around him and pull him tightly towards me. I feel him trembling slightly and as I look at him, I see that his cheeks are wet with tears.

"I've missed you son," I say, "I can't tell you how much I've missed you."

"I've missed you too, Dad, we were so worried about you. It's good to have you back Dad!"

❖ ❖ ❖

Josh and I had taken to walking along the Berwickshire coastal paths in the afternoons when the weather wasn't too harsh. The walking and scenery gave us something to focus on but still encouraged us to talk.

"Your Grampy used to take me along here when I was a boy," I told Josh, "I used to find it very therapeutic then, too. I felt that I was able to tell him anything along these coasts and that the sea and wind would listen to my woes and hold onto my secrets."

Josh stopped and looked out to the sea, it was calm today and seemingly ready to listen again.

"I know you enjoyed your life here with Grampy, but you also had some terrible times as a little boy too, didn't you? Grampy always said that one day you might tell me your story but that it was always your story to tell."

"I did Josh, and these paths have probably heard it all before. I need to tell you my story because it will help to explain a lot of things to you. It's a long and troublesome story, so are you prepared for this?"

"I am Dad, I need to know what happened."

"Well, here goes…"

And my story unfolds and with each word shared, my burden feels lighter.

❖❖❖

"So now that you know what my story is, I need to explain how it affected me and as a consequence, what happened to the two of us. As I tell you this though, you need to understand that my *behaviours* resulted from a defence mechanism from years of unresolved trauma and that in no way did I mean you any harm."

"Dad, I know you didn't mean any harm, I understand all that. I have spoken to Mum and Grampy and I do understand. And you talk about *'behaviours'* but can I say, I never felt harmed, so what you feel you have done or how you have *behaved*, hasn't actually happened, it was all contained within your own story, and within you. You hid it too well to be honest, we didn't realise there was a problem until it was too late."

Josh looked at me with genuine concern, but there was a shift in our relationship emerging. He was no longer the little boy and I was no longer just his father, this was now an adult-to-adult conversation. He nodded to me as an indication to continue and my heart filled with emotion and pride for my son as I carried on with my tale.

"Well Josh, you may not remember this particular day, but we had gone swimming, you were 13 at the time and on this particular day, everything seemed to change for me. I had a really vivid and traumatic flashback when we were in the changing rooms and I was finding it hard to breath. You were talking about your starring role as Puck in the school play but all I could think about was being back in my old school changing rooms. The smells, the noises, everything was trying to drag me back there."

"Yes, I do remember that, you said you had low blood sugar, but you were acting pretty weirdly at the time."

"I'm sure I must have been behaving very oddly! The consultant believes that it was from that point onwards that I started to project my own childhood fears onto you."

"I don't get it, what does that mean?"

"Basically, the fears that I had as a child were never addressed but locked away. That particular day, I looked at you and it suddenly dawned on me that you had become a teenager – not my little boy anymore but an adolescent. You had become the little boy that I was when I was attacked, in my mind you became Little Tim. From then on, all the fears that little Tim had were projected onto you. In my mind, it was you who was afraid of touch, of hugs, of human contact, of men in particular, I felt that I couldn't touch you in case you (or little Tim) thought I was a perpetrator, a predator. But there was another side to it, because in my mind, I had failed to protect Little Tim and failed to cry out for help, Little Tim had suffered. To compensate for this, I thought that I should be the one to protect you from everything and everybody. That night when I had my breakdown, I saw you arrive home with those bruises on your face and Lee's arm around you and I thought I had failed you, somehow, I had associated Lee as being someone who would exploit you and hurt you. In my mind, I had also failed you. I hadn't been able to protect you, or little Tim again, just like I hadn't been able to protect little Tim all those years ago when I couldn't cry out, or run away, or stop the attack. The night of the breakdown, I felt totally crushed, I couldn't breathe, I couldn't move. That's when I really thought I was going to die, I had gone into such a severe anxiety attack that I couldn't breathe, I had a crushing pain in my chest and I truly thought I was going to die."

"I had no idea that you were going through all that stress, it must have been a terrible time for you Dad. And to think that Lee and I would have been the catalyst for your breakdown, I can't believe it. I really can't believe this; I feel just terrible."

"Josh, I haven't told you this to make you feel responsible for it, I'm telling you this so that you understand why I behaved in the way I did. I need you to know that I am not homophobic, and that I have no problem with you being gay. I needed to tell you this story because of the issues I had with being sexually abused. In my head, the thought of you being penetrated by another man, or a man using you for sex was intolerable. It brought back too much trauma for me. It brought back the pain and fear and trauma that I had as a child. All those dreadful feelings, because I couldn't accept them as being part of me, were projected onto you and in my mind, you were experiencing those feelings and I had failed to protect you."

"I hope that can you understand that the way I behaved was because of my mental illness and trauma. In my head, the only image I wanted to keep of you was as my beautiful little boy in his Spiderman outfit, shooting imaginary spiderwebs and catching criminals. Anything else was beyond my reasoning. The thought of Lee in your life was just too much for me."

Josh was quiet for a while as we walked on.

"I can understand your anxiety Dad, but can I talk to you about me and Lee for a little bit and maybe that will help you?"

"Yes, please do, I hardly spoke to Lee when I did meet him so really know nothing about the poor boy. God knows what he thinks of me!"

Josh took a moment then continued.

"I think my relationship with Lee is very special. He is the first person I have ever had a relationship with, I didn't date any girls because I wasn't attracted to them and I found it very hard to date boys, partly because I didn't know how to ask a boy out, but mainly because I needed to know that there was a possible future in the relationship. I didn't want just a one-night-stand: I look at your relationship with Mum and I think it's a hard act to follow you know." Josh looked at me and we exchanged knowing smiles, before he continued.

"I know you have concerns about me being abused, but any sexual relationship needs to be based on mutual consent. Lee and I have an adult relationship and it is based on loving and mutual consent. It isn't abuse, it's not what happened to you. We love each other."

"If you liken it to a heterosexual couple, if a woman was attacked as a young girl by a man, when she grows up, she could still have a successful, healthy, loving, consensual relationship with another man. It would take time and probably lots of counselling and patience on both parts but it would be possible."

"The problem is that you made me into *Little Tim*, but you know I'm not really that person. You need to take a good look at me Dad and take away the picture of Little Tim that you see projected around me, because it's not really there." Josh stopped walking and turned to look at me putting his hands on my shoulders.

"Really look at me Dad, tell me exactly what you see."

Part of me didn't want to look at Josh because of the pain I had caused him, but I needed to go through this to get to where we needed to be. I looked at Josh with pride in my chest. He was wise beyond his years. I looked at him and took in all his features, and was reminded that when he was a child, how much he resembled Libby, but as I looked at him now there were so many features that looked familiar to me, so many things that took me back to my own childhood, that took me way, way back to before my school days, then it struck me why.

"For the first time, I can see that you that you have your grandmother's eyes. I have never noticed how much you take after her Josh. You remind me so much of her, I can actually remember the colour of her eyes now."

Josh smiled.

"OK, what else do you see?"

I shook myself away from the sudden memories of my Mama and looked at Josh again.

"I see a handsome young man who is wise beyond his years. But what's more important is what I don't see, I don't see a little boy, I don't see Little Tim. I see a strong character with a good sense of judgement, someone who I don't need to protect, but someone who I will always worry about because he is my son."

Josh smiled then lowered his arms and we continued with our walk.

"I guess that goes with the job description of parenting!" Josh said, then he added earnestly.

"And you do know by now that Lee would never do anything to hurt me, don't you Dad? Like I said, everything in our relationship is based on love and mutual understanding, so please don't worry about me in that way."

"Thank you, Josh. Everything you have told me today just really consolidates the work I've been doing with the consultant, but it's very good to hear this from you."

We continued our walk in companionable silence for a while, each of us with our own thoughts, the only sound was our shoes: a mesmerising pounding, crunching the gravel as we walked. Josh had really grown up in the last few months and I wasn't aware of how just much I had missed of his maturity.

"I'm very proud of you son, and Lee is a very lucky man! Speaking of Lee, how is he?"

"All good Dad, we're looking to share a flat next year with it being final's year. Megan might share with us but if not, it will just be the two of us."

"Well, you know the trust fund will support you, that's what it's for, you know? I've used hardly any of it so there's plenty for you to use if you want it."

"Yeah, thanks Dad, I appreciate that, but why was that? Why didn't you want to use the money?"

"I guess it was all part of burying my head in the sand. I didn't want to think of my father at all because it was a trigger for flashbacks but also it was a way of avoiding grieving for my parents. If I didn't use the money, I didn't have to think of them as being dead, so their money was just kept in Trust by Grandpa for all these years until we decided what to do with it all. And to be fair, we have had decent jobs and didn't need lots of money, we didn't go for fancy exotic holidays so we haven't missed it. We took out money from the trust to buy the house and we always said that your university would be paid for from the Trust but apart from that it's still intact."

"Well thanks again Dad, I appreciate it."

"Nice to know we didn't spoil you too!"

"Yeah, thanks for that too, Dad," Josh chuckled and rolled his eyes.

"Come on, let's get back to the house, they'll be wondering where we are. It's been a good day, we've sorted out a great deal and I need a hot cup of tea, and if I'm not wrong, there may be some of that nice carrot cake left over!" Josh laughed and rolled his eyes.

"I've never known anyone with such a sweet tooth as you Dad!"

❖❖❖

# 23
# Libby – Birmingham, September, 2018

Thirty years? I'm looking in the mirror and see my reflection as I'm shaking my head at the impossibility of it. It was 30 years ago this month that I moved down from Cupar to Birmingham as a 23-year-old.

I don't have a problem with ageing really, but I'm just taken aback at how old I actually am and it does take me by surprise me when I hear my age out loud, like the other day when I went for my Mammogram. After I gave my date of birth, the nurse made a quick calculation and said: "So that makes you 53?" *What a lot of years*, I thought! So yes, it does surprise me that I'm getting on a bit!

I still think of Josh as being very young, and yet, at his age, I had lived in Edinburgh for five years, moved down to Birmingham, was even engaged. I think I'm finding it hard to move from the parent-child relationship with Josh, I know I still feel very protective of him, but when I think of how he handled everything when Grampy died, he was incredibly strong and capable. In fact, I would say he was the one who kept the whole family together.

Poor Grampy, what a difficult time that was for everyone. He didn't quite get to his 100$^{th}$ birthday, and he had been terribly frail for a number of years, but it was a peaceful death, as if that could help anyone get over something like that. Grampy was the glue that held the family together. I was so worried about Tim at the time, but all the therapy that he had previously, obviously helped him get through it.

He and Josh worked through everything with the family solicitor, and they had the agonising decision as to what to do about Sandstone. With all the death duties and inheritance tax to pay, it was an expensive property to keep. Without opening it up to the public or turning it into a hotel, it would have been impossible to maintain it. And it's not as though the house was of huge historical importance, and whilst there were some nice pieces of art, there were no real crowd pullers like a Rubens or a Turner that would entice lots of people to queue up and visit the property. Josh and Lee did consider going into business together and opening it as a luxury guesthouse, but their hearts weren't really in it, and I'm not sure that's what Grampy would really have wanted. So it was with a really heavy heart that the decision was made to sell the property.

Tim really is in a good place right now, I haven't seen him so well for a long time, and his relationship with Josh is just wonderful. They are in Scotland on a boys' walking holiday this week. I just love that they have that connection now, five years ago, that would have been out of the question.

Josh still loves Manchester and seems to be making that his home, with Lee of course. They are such a good couple together. I miss them though, but who am I to complain, how many miles away from my dad did I move?

I do feel blessed though, I still manage to fill my days; I'm not entirely sure how, because I definitely don't do a fraction of the things that I used to do, but I keep myself busy. I've discovered that I enjoy gardening, and that I can actually cook, so all the years of convenience foods are now a thing of the past. I've also joined the local tennis club which is a 25-minute walk from where we live.

I never actually returned to work after leaving the bank in April 2009, I didn't want the constant battle with having to fight my corner for every scrap of promotion. It also meant that I was able to put the past behind me and start afresh.

I decided to volunteer for a homeless charity in Moseley once a week instead of working, it can be quite challenging at times, but it keeps me grounded. It has given me a new set of friends and a different outlook on life in comparison to the tennis and banking crowd that I generally socialise with.

But this week, with Tim on his boys' holiday, it's a quiet week at home, with the occasional game of mixed doubles. The weather continues to be hot even, after the incredible heatwave of the summer, and the garden is keeping me busy.

❖❖❖

# 24
# Josh – The Highlands, September, 2018

"I've heard that there's a great little cafe in Kincraig that's recently opened up and it's supposed to sell the best cakes in the area."

"Dad! That's outrageous! How can you possibly know that? Is there any cake shop in the whole of the UK that you don't know about?"

"I have my ear to the ground Josh, but I can't reveal my sources!"

We both laughed but agreed that a hot coffee and a cake before our walk would be a good idea.

But seriously, Dad *was* outrageous! He never could resist anything sweet. As we reached the small cafe, it already looked quite busy but we had arrived just as the lunchtime rush was starting. For such a tiny little village, it was a busy cafe. As we walked in, I caught the first few bars of a well-known song and it made me smile.

"Well this is definitely my kind of place Dad!"

He looked at me quizzically, then laughed at me dancing with my index fingers in the air pointing to the beat of the music as I started singing along.

"This is one of the great floor-fillers in Via," I said to Dad, thinking of my favourite gay club in Manchester, then carried on singing.

Dad guffawed, it was so good to see him laugh and enjoy himself, a few years ago, he would have been horrified to think of me in a gay club.

"The Village People, 1978 I think, I was about 15 at the time!"

"Good knowledge Dad! You should come clubbing with us sometime!" Dad looked at me sceptically then winked.

"YMCA and a bit of Dad dancing at Via, that would be something to behold!" He was still laughing but shaking his head at the thought of it.

"Mmmm, maybe not then," I agreed.

"Table for two, is it?" The young waiter asked, then showed us to our table, it was a really small cafe with only eight or nine tables in total and we took the last table. We had intended to just have coffee and cake, but the filled focaccia on the menu looked too good to miss out on so we each ordered one, followed by coffee and (I had to agree) the most delicious-looking cakes.

The cafe's playlist continued with a '70s vibe and Dad visibly cringed as he heard the next song. "Bay City Rollers: '75 or possibly '76, I would have been about 12 at the time, your mum loved them as a wee girl!"

"I didn't know you were such an expert in popular music Dad. I don't think I've ever heard you play a radio in your life!"

Dad's face clouded over a little and I could see he was distracted for a while. I placed my hand on his elbow gently.

"What are you thinking Dad, you seem miles away."

Dad patted my hand, an easy gesture, that communicated so much. It had become so familiar to me now, but a gesture which a few years ago we would never have shared.

"No, you're right Josh, I never listened to music on the radio; I made sure I avoided it. It was one of the strategies I had for managing my flashbacks, if I heard *that particular song* then it could trigger a panic attack, so I just stopped listening to music. So yes, you're right, we never had a radio on in the house. But I can listen to music from those times now and I don't have the same anxieties and now that my head is clearer, I seem to have a better memory for the bands and titles of songs too. But it does make me sad to think that this is another thing in your life that you missed out on because of my illness, that we never shared music or favourite songs together."

"Dad, I don't think that I've missed out on anything at all, you've got to stop thinking like this. I know that in your mind, you think you withdrew from me when I was a teenager, but teenage boys find it really embarrassing to hug their fathers anyway so it wasn't something that I actually noticed until I was about 16 or 17 anyway. And if you think that we would have shared a favourite song – come on – The Bay City Rollers! Do you really think that we would have had the same taste in music?" I said this laughing with him, hoping to lighten the mood; I didn't want Dad dragged back to the memory of his illness.

It had the intended effect, and we were both exchanging jibes about each other's taste in music as our enormous focaccia arrived, they would fill us up for the whole day.

As we waited for our coffee, we looked at the guidebook for local walks.

"So, there's the Ben Macdui walk if you're up for it Dad? Let's have a look at what it says. Ben Macdui means the hill of Macduff. Did you know that this hill is supposed to have a ghost? *The Big Grey Man* – apparently he's supposed to follow climbers off the hill, he's Scotland's answer to the Yeti. It says here: '*Heard more often than seen but described as a threatening figure.*'"

Dad thought about it for a minute.

"I think that's quite a long walk isn't it? And looking at the weather forecast, I'm not sure we'll have time to do Ben Macdui today. We'd end up having to stay in the Corrour Bothy if we get caught up in bad weather, and we're not equipped for that sort of walk today. Perhaps we should save that for another day and go for a shorter walk?"

I looked back at the guidebook again and flicked through the pages.

"What about The Ryvoan Bothy Walk, we haven't done that one for a while, and we can do that in an afternoon?"

Our coffees arrived, but the cakes were too much even for Dad so we asked for the cakes 'to go' and got some extra coffees in our travel mugs.

❖❖❖

The Ryvoan Bothy walk was a circular walk and we decided to do the route anti-clockwise so that we had the longer section with no incline before tackling the steeper part, primarily to digest the enormous lunch we had just eaten.

We parked in Glenmore Lodge Visitor Centre and took the path towards the Green Lochan and then onto the Bothy. The sun was hitting the Lochan as we passed it and it looked magical, the water was the colour of deep turquoise, tinged with green from the algae in the water. Although the guidebook did give us an alternative rationale for the colour. Legend had it that the Lochan took on the colour because pixies washed their socks in it!

The path was good and it took us less than an hour to get to the Bothy. As we entered the Bothy, we could smell the smoke from the previous night's log fire, it was very primitive accommodation with just a few pots and pans (of questionable cleanliness); a table and a few chairs, most of which were heavily repaired using gaffer tape. The sleeping arrangement was a long wooden bench, and someone had already left their backpack to stake their claim to the bed for the night and gone off hiking. The toilet arrangement was a spade with a polite notice requesting that guests were, '*never to use the vicinity of the bothy as a toilet, and to bury all human waste.*'

I chuckled to myself and Dad turned to see what had amused me.

"Lee would be horrified with this!" I pointed at the notice. "I think I'll send a picture of the spade and this notice to him just to see what he says."

In the caption box, I added:

*Toilet facilities on walk*
*Bit primitive*
*Lol* ☺
*xx*

"I can't get a strong enough signal to send the picture, I guess he'll get it at some point though."

I thought about the Bothy and having to sleep there, and I really wouldn't fancy it myself if I was honest! Lee might be a bit snooty about hotels, but I had to agree with him on this one!

My phone must have picked up a signal and sent the picture because a text arrived from Lee just then:

*OMG!*
*Don't they have any 5\**
*Hotels in Scotland?*
*;) xx*

I chuckled and read it out loud to Dad.

"I have to agree with him, you know Dad, it's less than an hour's walk away from a main road and numerous hotels, you'd have to be desperate to want to stay here!"

"Lots of people are happy to stay in Bothy's Josh, and you would be glad of the shelter in a bad storm. There's a real kudos in staying in as many Bothies as possible, lots of people tick them off as they stay in them, although, I have to agree with you, at my age I think I would prefer a hotel too!"

"Come on Dad, you're not old, you're still young and fitter than a lot of people my age that's for sure."

"Thanks son! I'm surprised you actually got a signal here though. I'll need to give your mum a ring when we get back to the Visitor Centre, I haven't spoken to her all day."

It was nice to hear Dad talking about Mum that way, and as walking had become our way of sharing things so I felt comfortable asking Dad about his feelings.

"Do you miss Mum when you're away?"

"That's a good question, I do miss her, and I miss hearing her voice, but I think I miss her more if she goes away, rather than when I'm away with you. That probably sounds a bit selfish, but if I'm the one left at home, then I feel lonely, and I miss her more. I worry about her when I leave her on her own, I suppose."

We leave the Bothy and start towards the steeper section of the walk. There's a steep zig-zag path leading towards the summit, the guidebook gives its Gaelic name as *Meal a'Bhuachaille* meaning *'Hill of the Heardsman'* or *Shepherd's Hill*. The purple of the heather is breathtaking, and as we pause and turn around to catch our breath, we take in the view of the Bothy and Loch Morlich in the distance.

I think of my mum and dad being together for all those years. They've been together for 30 years but I'm sure they met a few years before then.

"How did you and Mum actually meet?"

Dad smiled at the thought.

"We bumped into each other a few times in Edinburgh, but never really got to know each other. The first time was at a bus stop, then it was at a Bowie concert, then bizarrely, a friend brought her to a cricket match that I was playing in. Grandpa was spectating and she ended up talking to him all day, not knowing that I was playing. Your grampy introduced us at the end of the game. After the match, I gave her a lift home, we had planned to go on another date, but she left Edinburgh suddenly after her mum died and I didn't see her again for five years until I bumped into her on a train to Birmingham. It was as though fate had taken control of our lives and kept trying to push us together."

"That's really romantic!"

"Yes, I suppose it is! But, after that, I made sure she never left my side!"

"How did you know though? How did you know she was the one for you, of all the girls in the world?"

"I just did, I can't tell you how I knew. It's not as though I dated lots of girls though. When you're given a nickname of '*Tiddler*', it doesn't fill you with much confidence when it comes to dating girls let me tell you! But there was something about your Mum from the very first time I met her at the bus stop that I was attracted to and I really wanted to get to know her. The trouble was that things just kept getting in the way and we couldn't seem to make it happen. It took us five years to finally make it happen."

The zigzag path was getting steeper and our breathing was more laboured, with the path also veering into a single track, it made conversation much harder. We were both quiet for a while, taking in the scenery and left to our own thoughts. For me, it was thinking about Lee and our relationship. We were very happy together, and recently Lee had been hinting about, a civil partnership or marriage, but neither of us had actually proposed yet.

Then the path widened a little and we were able to resume our conversation.

"Did you always know you wanted to marry Mum?"

"I guess so, it was always a progression of our relationship."

"Is that how you see marriage? As a progression to a relationship?"

"No, not necessarily Josh, marriage is a contract, a promise if you like. You make the promise legally so it's a legal contract. Some people make this promise in front of

God, to whichever God their faith follows, but it is still a legal contract that says you promise to stay with that person or love, honour and cherish that person, or whatever vows you decide upon. If you are ready to make that commitment to that person, then yes, you could see it as a progression of the relationship."

"Yeah, I get that, it makes sense, but I think I have a problem with this legal contract."

"Really? Why is that?"

"Well, we make contracts for all sorts of things in life, and we can find ways of getting out of them. People can always get a solicitor or barrister to find some sort of loophole to get out of the contract. It happens all the time when you think of how many divorces there are these days. So, you get married; make a legal contract; and you change your mind or find a better offer and get some legal bod to get you out of it. But if you really, really love somebody, it's not just about breaking a contract, if you break up a marriage, what you are really doing is breaking someone's heart. What you really should be asking yourself is, am I ready to commit to this person and at the risk of all else, promise to never break their heart? Because that's what it boils down to isn't it? And if that's the case, why do you need a legal contract to do that?"

Dad was quiet for a little while, but he nodded so I knew he was thinking this over.

We had to navigate over a rocky section that once again had veered into a single track so we couldn't continue with this exchange for a while. It gave me time to reflect on the words that I had voiced though, I hadn't realised that I had harboured those feelings about marriage. I didn't think that I was against marriage, it was just that I wanted it to be for the right reasons and not just to get that piece of paper or for a tax break.

We were getting closer to the summit now and the wind was whipping across the top. The views were stunning though and the weather was holding out. Ahead, I could see the Cairn, the mound of stones that marked the summit, and I could see the path widening. We usually took shelter from the wind behind the Cairn so we may well be able to admire the view with our takeaway coffees.

We arrived at the summit, and the wind was biting, so we didn't stay too long to admire the views of Loch Morlich and the Cairngorms, but set off down the other side, which was not such a steep incline as the ascent.

"You seem a bit quiet Dad, are you thinking about Mum?"

"I am, but I'm also thinking about what you said about marriage. It's an interesting point, and a very noble attitude. I'm just wondering if, in all the 30 years of marriage, I can hand on heart say that I have never done anything that would have broken your mum's heart. I would never have done anything intentionally, but with my illness, I know that she had such a lot to deal with. Did she ever feel that it was too much? Did she ever feel that she wanted to walk away from the marriage?"

"I suppose what I'm trying to say is that we all start off by telling ourselves that we will never break the heart of the person we love and we say that with every good intention. But what if people change? What if both people change? What if you have a situation where one person is more dominant than the other and takes advantage, and the weaker person then can't get out of the relationship. If you have a legal contract of marriage, then that can help the weaker person in these situations because the promise to *love, honour and cherish* has been broken. So, it's not a loophole that the solicitor is looking for, it's a broken vow."

"OK, yeah, I get that. I guess I'm a bit naïve really. It's not something that I've had to think about before, but you never know!"

"So, are you and Lee thinking about making that commitment now?"

"We have skirted around the subject, but we haven't really had the conversation. It's good to talk it through with you, the problem is you and Mum have this strong bond, and whatever you say about her feeling it was too much, you can forget that, she will never walk away from you."

"It's good that you are really taking it seriously Josh, marriage is a very serious business and as you say, so many people rush into it and don't consider that life isn't always a bed of roses. It's too easy sometimes to forget to be considerate towards each other when you've been together for many years, then you end up taking each other for granted, and that causes resentment.

It's something that you need to talk to each other about though, and explore your own strengths and coping strategies, because there will be hard times, and you will need to support each other."

"Wow, that was a bit deep! How did we get onto that one? But thanks Dad! You're right. I think Grampy might have rubbed off onto you because you're sounding a bit like him at the moment!"

"Well, you couldn't give me a better compliment Josh!"

We were reaching the lower part of the mountain and were approaching the forest path that would eventually lead back to the car park so we were getting toward the end of our walk. Dad was looking towards the sky; it did look like the weather was about to change for the worse. The grey, heavy-looking clouds were much lower now and we couldn't see the summit of Shepherd's Hill any longer.

"Not far now then Dad?"

"Good job, looking at that rain cloud, we'll probably make it back without having to put our waterproof trousers on if we speed up a bit."

Dad was waiting for me in the Glenmore Visitor Centre Cafe as I came out of the gents.

"Absolutely no signal on my phone whatsoever, I tried to call your mum using the payphone but she's not picking up. Do you need anything to drink or shall we just head on back to the B&B? I've got some bottles of water in the car if you're thirsty, but if you want a coffee or anything to eat, we can grab something here?"

"I'm not hungry at all Dad, I can wait till this evening for Dinner. I might have a bottle of water in the car though. Let's get back to the B&B, I could do with a hot shower. There's Wi-Fi there too so you'll be able to message or FaceTime Mum."

# 25
# Libby – Birmingham, September, 2018

It had been another hot day and I had just finished deadheading and weeding in the garden. I had come inside to cool down and grab a cold drink when I heard my mobile phone ring and thought it must be Tim. I looked at the number, it wasn't a number I recognised but I answered it anyway just in case it was important.

"Hello, Libby Ashford Speaking."

"Hello Libby Ashford," the voice on the other end replied. I didn't recognise the voice at all, it was a female voice and she sounded quite disgruntled but I couldn't fathom why. I spoke again: "Hello, who is this, how can I help you?"

"Who is this, how can I help you?" she replied.

The woman was trying to mimic my voice, I couldn't understand what this was about but clearly it was a crank call so I decided to end it.

"I'm sorry but I think you must have the wrong number so I'm going to hang up now."

Before I had the chance to hang up, she launched into a tirade with a viciousness that completely floored me.

"I know who you are Libby Ashford and I know what you did. You think you are so high and mighty, but you are nothing but a SLUT."

I stood there with the phone in my hand and felt like a fist had punched me in the stomach. Time stood still and the blood froze in my veins. Then my heart started pounding, followed closely with a pounding in my head, and I could feel the pulse beat in my neck as she continued.

"You have ruined my life and now I am going to ruin yours. I have proof of what you did, I have the photograph he took. You didn't know did you? He told me you didn't know about it."

"What are you talking about? Who is this?" I fumbled, flustered now.

"I am Graham's WIFE."

And with that she cut me off.

I sat there, trembling, unable to think. And then my phone pinged again, this time with a text.

*I know who you are*
*and I know what you did.*
*You think you are so high*
*and mighty but you are*
*nothing but a SLUT!*

Then the phone pinged again and a photograph that I didn't even know existed popped onto my screen. It was a semi naked photograph of me. I was lying on a bed in a hotel room, with a sheet covering most of me but baring my leg and my breast. I recoiled in horror. I felt a hot burning shame rise through me to my neck and face. I knew that this day would come back to haunt me.

How could I have been so stupid? How could I have let myself down? How could I have let myself get into such a position? It was years ago now, but I still felt the shame and humiliation of it all so clearly.

It was in 2008, RBS shares had dropped by 35%. This was at the start of the problems for the bank.

The chancellor of the time, Alistair Darling had been asked by RBS for loans to bail out the bank.

It started with £20B in October but there were rumours that even that would not help the bank and that a second bailout would be needed the following year. The department managers were all called in for a crisis meeting at the end of the day. Afterwards we just sat there stunned until one of the managers suggested we all go for a drink to drown our sorrows. I remember that I had phoned Tim and told him that we had a crisis meeting going on but he said he was at home so wasn't a problem if I was late home from work.

There were four of us drinking to start with, then just two of us, myself and Doreen, the only other female manager in the bank at the time. We were discussing how likely it was that they would keep two senior female managers with all the cutbacks that were happening, when Graham joined us from out of nowhere. Graham was Doreen's assistant manager, a highflyer and a real charmer. He was a ladies' man, extremely attractive but dangerous with it, he was exactly the sort of man who I would have avoided if I was single or out on my own, but with Doreen's company, I felt safe. He had offered to buy us a round of drinks and we accepted thinking one more on a work night would be acceptable. Things got a little blurry but I remember Doreen leaving and Graham saying he would get a taxi for me. The next thing I knew, we were kissing in the back of the taxi and he was asking if I wanted to go somewhere private. In my stupid drunken state, I agreed and we ended up at the Malmaison Hotel in the Mailbox of all places. Not very discreet at all, we could have bumped into anybody in that area.

I have very little recollection of anything after arriving at Malmaison until I woke up at 1:30 am and found myself naked on the bed. I was horrified at what I had done, mortified. Flashbacks of the evening kept coming back to me in a hazy memory and I felt physically sick, not just because of the alcohol but because of what I must have done in such a drunken state.

I knew I had to get home, but I would have to brazen it out and get reception to find a taxi for me. A lone woman leaving a hotel at 1:30 am – they would know what that meant! How did I get myself into this situation?

When I eventually did get home, it was after 2:30 am. I think Tim was asleep, he didn't stir when I got into bed, but I can't be sure. He hasn't said anything to this day and I haven't said anything either. It has been my guilty secret ever since. Another secret in this family that runs deep and may yet be the one thing that destroys us.

Graham tried to speak to me about it the next day at work but I tried to pull rank. I told him that if he ever spoke about it again to anybody, I would find a way to discredit him, that he would never get promotion at this bank. But he looked at me, directly in my eyes and said with a smirk on his face, "Somehow, Mrs A, I don't think you will be able to do that!"

I thought that he was calling my bluff and that he knew that personnel would not allow me to override a decision that they had made, but I meant it, I would have tried to get him out of the branch, but then the redundancy programme came out and it was me who jumped ship and I never thought I would have to see him again.

❖ ❖ ❖

My mobile phone rings again and startles me. I look at the number, I think it's the same number as previously. I'm unsure whether to answer it or not, but in the end, I do, immediately regretting it.

"So, you've received my messages then?" The woman's tone was bitter, it was hardly surprising in the circumstances, but why did Graham keep the picture for nine years? What did he think he would do with this?

He must have kept it thinking he could use it against anything I might have done to him. That must have been why he was so confident and smirking at me when I tried to pull rank on him back then.

I brought myself back to the phone call.

"Look, I don't know what you think is going on, but I can assure you there is nothing going on at all. I don't know how your husband got that photograph, and I didn't even know it existed. Now I think you should stop phoning me and leave me alone."

"You really think that's it? You sleep with my husband and I should just leave you alone? You have ruined my life. I know everything about you Libby Ashford, so I am going to ruin your life. I'm going to send this photograph to your husband and he will know what a slut you really are."

And then she again cuts me off, leaving me shaking and trembling, terrified as to whether she really does know everything about me and whether she can get hold of Tim's number to send the evidence to him.

My mobile phone rings again, but this time I don't answer it. I don't recognise the number and I can't face speaking to that woman again. It goes through to answerphone and a couple of moments later I get a message to say I have a missed call and voicemail. I really don't want to hear what that woman has to say, but I can't leave it on my phone, so I click on the message.

It's from Tim. He tells me that there is no signal where he is because of bad weather, he's calling from a payphone in a coffee shop, and that he misses me.

I sit at the table with my head in my hands, feeling shame and guilt, not knowing what I can do. God, what a mess. How could I have done this to Tim? What a bloody mess.

I try to think of who might be able to help me but I am too ashamed to ask anyone for help so I know I will have to sort this out myself. I have two days before Tim gets home and I need to get this sorted out before then. The first thing I need to do is get hold of Graham and find out what he did.

After a sleepless night, first thing in the morning I call the bank and ask to be put through to the manager of business banking. When asked who was calling, I merely tell them it's a personal call. Thankfully I had kept in touch with Doreen from the bank and was up to date with who had been given promotion – including Graham so I knew where he was based. When he answered, it took everything I had to keep my temper in check, but I managed to be courteous.

"Libby, I thought you might call," his attitude was so casual that I could no longer keep hold of my anger.

"How dare you! I have had your wife contact me with an extremely sensitive photograph. Firstly, you had no right to take that photograph without my permission, and secondly you had no right to keep it. How did your wife get hold of it and how did she get my number?"

Graham had the decency to sound mildly contrite but not contrite enough as far as I was concerned. "I know, I shouldn't have taken it, but you looked sweet when you were sleeping. I forgot I had it to be honest and I kept it on my phone with your phone number. My wife picked up my phone when I accidentally left it at home one day and she went through all the contacts. That's when she found it. She's just mad at me that's all."

"WHAT! Why did you keep my photograph, and why did you have my phone number? I don't believe a word that you have said. You were planning to use this in case I blocked your progress, weren't you? This was why you were always so smug, wasn't it? Your wife is threatening to use this to ruin my life so you need to talk to her and make peace with her and make sure she doesn't keep harassing me. Do you understand?"

"OK, I'll do my best. Look I have a call waiting so I need to go but I'll talk to her, OK?"

"You better had Graham or you will hear from me again. Let's hope this is the last time we need to speak to each other. Goodbye Graham."

I was shaking with anger when I got off the phone and the anger brought with it tears of frustration. How dare he? He had absolutely no right. There must be laws against this surely?

It didn't take me long to find out the answer to that, a quick search on Google informed me that indecent images taken without permission were a breach of privacy laws. Well, I thought, if he doesn't do anything to stop this immediately, I will definitely do something about that.

Just then my mobile phone rang. I looked at the number, feeling paralysed with fear. Should I answer it in case it was Tim again or just ignore it. In the end, I answered it and cursed myself for doing so; the woman on the end of the line began her tirade of insults again: "You were talking to my husband again weren't you, slut."

I had had enough, I cut the call and blocked the number so I wouldn't have to take any more calls from her, then immediately called Graham again. His response was pitiful.

"I'm trying to make her see sense, but she's just not listening to me."

I can't believe that I could ever have found this weak, spineless excuse of a man even remotely attractive. My patience was running very thin and I could feel my hackles rising. It was a long time since I had reprimanded anybody, but I was so angry with him that I could no longer be polite towards him.

"Well Graham, you need to man-up and try harder. If I have one more call from her, then I will take further action."

And with that I hung up on him before I could say anything further that I might really regret.

My mobile phone rang again, I was trembling with anxiety as I picked it up, but when I looked at the number, it was Tim's. I answered it with relief.

"Are you OK Libby? You sound really tense?"

I swallowed back tears of frustration; I couldn't cry now or Tim would want to know why I was crying. Thinking quickly, I told Tim I had stubbed my toe on the table leg and I tried to laugh it off. We had a long chat and caught up on the last couple of days, it was nice to talk about their trip.

I was trying hard to forget about that woman, but she was always in the back of my mind and I was finding it hard to relax and act normally. In the end, I said I had a game of Tennis Doubles booked so needed to dash, I had a quick chat with Josh who said they would call after their walk if they had a good enough signal or could call from the hotel phone if not.

It was lunchtime and I realised that I hadn't eaten anything since my lunch yesterday. I was so consumed and wrapped up with this unwelcome situation that the thought of food made me feel nauseous. I opened the fridge door and peered in but nothing took my fancy. The cupboard was equally uninspiring: I saw some oatcakes, a throwback from my childhood. Maybe I could have those with some cheese? No, I couldn't face that either. I drank some water and sat at the kitchen table.

I was weary from tension and lack of food and sleep. I sat back in the chair and tried to calm myself, closing my eyes and trying to rest, but I kept seeing that photograph in my mind's eye. Opening my eyes I gazed upon the picture on the wall, it was a framed print of Rossetti's *Proserpine,* Tim bought it for me when we moved into the house as a gift. It was the same picture that I bought as a poster for my flat on the first day I moved to Birmingham. It made me smile to think of Tim and that first day we spent together, then a wave of guilt swept over me again. How could I have done this to Tim? He was so kind and had gone through so much. I couldn't sit still, I became restless and started pacing, the anxiety building up in me. I took myself into the garden thinking that if I did have any energy I may as well spend it doing something useful so I start hoeing the beds that I had weeded yesterday, but all the time my mind was thinking about that woman. What if she did manage to send the picture to Tim? Maybe I should just talk to him about it. Tell him how it happened. I was drunk after all. Graham must have taken advantage of me; I couldn't even remember any of what happened. Did he put something in my drink? One minute I was fine and talking to Doreen and the next, everything was just a blur. It was so long ago now; I can't actually remember any details. Or was I just kidding myself, trying to make excuses for myself? I do remember kissing him, and I vaguely remember agreeing to go somewhere else with him. I can't tell Tim that, can I? I don't know what to do, my mind was in a whirl, with arguments for and against telling Tim going around and around in circles.

The weather was changing, dark clouds had gathered to match my mood. According to the Met Office, the long hot summer that we had enjoyed and the warm September was about be replaced by some welcome rain. The grass was very dry and yellow so the garden would benefit from the rain even if the sunbathers in Cannon Hill Park didn't relish it.

I felt better having spent an afternoon in the garden, but needed to eat something, so again looked in the fridge and found some vegetables and salmon that would stir fry quickly with some noodles, without too much effort.

As I ate my simple supper, the rain was pouring down, clearing the air. It felt less oppressive now – I hoped that this was a metaphor for my unwanted situation.

After a long hot shower, I start to relax a little for the first time in 24 hours. I check my phone to see if Tim has called and find that I have voicemail so click to listen to the message: "You've been talking to my husband again, haven't you slut? He won't do what you say because he only listens to me."

I can't believe that she is still calling me! Using a different number! How many numbers would I have to block before she stops calling me? I delete the message immediately then check the time, 6:15, it's still possible that Graham would be in the office. Picking up my laptop, I bring up my mail server and type in Graham's work email address, knowing full well that he will not want anybody from work to see this email, he would deal with this as soon as possible:

Subject: HARASSMENT AND BREACH OF PRIVACY LAWS.

Graham,

As discussed previously, the continued harassment, texts, phone calls and abuse must stop with immediate effect. You will be aware of the breach of privacy laws involved with all of the above including the taking of indecent images without permission. Please be clear that I will not tolerate this and will have no hesitation in reporting this to both the bank and the police if there is *any* further harassment from *any* party.

Yours,

Elizabeth Ashford.

Sure enough, within minutes I have a single word reply back from him.

Subject: Re: HARASSMENT AND BREACH OF PRIVACY LAWS.

Understood.

I hope that this is enough to put a stop to this ghastly situation because I really don't want to go to the bank or the police, I just couldn't bear for it to go public, but I'm sure that he would not want the bank to find out that he has broken the law either. It's a game of *Chicken,* and about who will back down first. Let's hope both Graham and his wife back down for everyone's sake.

I was still very much on edge though, especially when Tim came home. He thought I looked very tense and tired. I told him I'd had trouble sleeping in the heat. What else could I tell him?

Days went by then weeks, and then a couple of months and I heard nothing from that woman and I started to relax a bit. But every time my phone pings or rings with an unknown number I still tense up. I have set my phone to '*silent for unknown numbers*' which causes a little frustration for deliveries if they try to call my number but eases the tension a bit.

I haven't mentioned it to Tim, it's still my secret. It's the only secret I've ever kept from him and I am wracked with guilt about it. I wish that I could remember more about the event, but it was so long ago and I was so drunk that I can't be sure what happened. I should have confronted Graham years ago, but I was so ashamed at the time I just wanted to forget about it and make it disappear. I can understand how poor Tim felt as a child after his trauma and not wanting people to know about his secret. Now that I have to live with my secret, I think I understand him even more. But I have to try and bury my own guilt and my secret as best as I can and live with this.

# Epilogue

*Libby: Birmingham, July 2019*

A long hot shower had revived me a little and I felt a bit more human when I emerged, finding a tall glass of water and some paracetamol waiting for me by my bed, at least someone in this house was sympathetic to my needs and my hangover. I'm guessing it would be Josh, or maybe even his old friend Megan from uni who had stayed over last night too.

I smile to myself when I think of my *'little' boy* being engaged. It had been on the cards for a while now, Tim told me that he and Josh had a long and meaningful talk about marriage and the whole concept of what it means when they were on their boys' walking holiday last year. I loved the fact that they were so close that they could talk about things like that now. It could all have been so different, we have been through such a lot as a family, Tim has worked hard to get over his childhood trauma and Josh has been incredibly understanding, he really is wise beyond his years.

I hear some raucous laughter coming from downstairs and quickly finish getting dressed.

My mobile phone pings with a message from Megan. I glance at the message but I only see the first two lines on the banner, before the screen goes black again. I pick up my phone and head downstairs. I am halfway downstairs and I lift my phone to look at the message again, the screen lights up and the message banner is visible. Two lines stand out with alarming clarity, all the other words are just a blur.

*secret from us all!*
*All over FB by now!*

A secret? All over Facebook? What was this about? What did this mean? My legs could no longer hold me and I sat on the stairs with a thud, just staring that the message. Images of the previous night were bombarding my brain, but I had no idea what this could be, other than…God, no!

Please no! I held my hands up to my face. Please don't let that awful picture have resurfaced again, and on Facebook? I wracked my brain again but nothing else would surface. What did Megan's message say? I looked at the message again and saw the text in its entirety.

*Thnx 4 letting us stay over.*
*Soz but had 2 go, fun night tho!*
*BTW, U a dark horse! Kept it*
*secret from us all!*
*Didn't know U had it in U*
*All over FB by now!*
*Luv ya xx*

A dark horse.
Kept it a secret.
All over Facebook.
No! Please God, not that photograph! But what else can it be?

"Oh, there you are Mibs, we thought we might have to send out a search party for you! Oh good grief, are you OK, you do look very pale, you look like you're having a hangover relapse!" Lee came to sit beside me. He really was a very sweet and caring young man. He had taken to calling me Mibs because he couldn't quite bring himself to call me mum and didn't want to call me Libby so this was his own way of being part of the family.

He looked at the phone in my hand and I tried to hide the message, but he said gently to me.

"So, Megan has let the cat out of the bag has she?"

My shoulders slumped forward and I held my head in my hands.

"I feel so ashamed Lee, I can't believe this is all over Facebook, how am I going to face Tim now? I thought I would never have to tell him."

"Hey, don't be so hard on yourself, there's plenty of people who have had a few drinks and let their guard down."

Lee put his arm around me and gave my shoulders a squeeze, I didn't understand how he could be so reasonable about this, he was so unconditionally accepting of everything and everybody, and so calming.

"Do you want to have a look at Facebook and see what people are saying about it? It's had a lot of comments, so you should be proud of yourself!"

I was absolutely horrified!

"Lee, you can't be serious! No, Please don't!"

But he was taking out his phone and opening up his Facebook app.

"Here it is, look, you're quite a star!"

I heard the song before I saw the video. It was the Shania Twain song that had been in my head all morning. Lee turned his phone towards me and showed me a video clip of me with an unknown man dancing a rather spectacular Cha Cha Cha to the song. I hadn't danced like that since I was 15, I had given up dancing just before my O'Grades because the practice was taking up too much time. The man was obviously taking the lead, but I must have dredged some memory for the dance from somewhere because we were doing a very good job. This couple were having fun, they were flirtatious, playful and full of energy. Everyone in the room was looking at them, clapping and cheering them on.

I sat on the stairs with my mouth open, gaping at the video clip, I looked at Lee.

"Is this what Meg was talking about?" I said, "Is this what she meant about me being a dark horse and keeping it a secret from everyone?"

"Well, nobody knew you could dance like that, not even Josh, he was as surprised as anyone! You were an absolute star, like Megan said, we didn't know you had it in you!"

A flood of relief washed over me, followed very closely by remorse and the sense of guilt that I still carried within me about the incident that happened ten years ago now. I still really need to talk to Tim about this, because I can't go on with this hanging over me and be panicking every time an unexpected situation like this occurs.

We heard the now very familiar opening bars of the Shania Twain song coming from the kitchen and the opening line being sung by Josh: "Let's go Girls!"

As we made our way to the kitchen, I was faced with a giant Shania look-alike in drag. I wondered if the day could get any more bizarre but howled with laughter at the sight of Tim dressed as Shania Twain.

"What on earth is going on?"

"Dad's found his inner Shania and didn't want to be outdone by you, so if you could take a seat please Mum, the show's about to begin!"

I really couldn't believe my eyes. Tim had really gone all out to dress as Shania, including the knee-high boots, short tight dress, top hat with a net veil and a long black coat. His make-up was very professionally done too.

The opening bars of the song started again and Tim started his performance.

It was the funniest thing I had ever seen him do, and all captured on my iPhone, including a couple of twirls and dips with Josh and Lee at the end.

The story behind the performance was that Tim had already seen the Facebook post of my dance and felt really guilty at having missed the best part of the evening. It turned out that a colleague of his was a part-time Shania drag artist and offered to lend him the costume, do his makeup, and show him a couple of moves to surprise us all this morning. It definitely did surprise us and to see him in his inner Shania was something to behold.

I looked at the last still picture I took of Tim with his arms around the two boys and I thought back to the day of his breakdown. We couldn't have come further as a family, and having secrets was no way for a family to thrive. I needed to tell Tim about my secret, I couldn't face him finding out from someone else, or worse still, from seeing a picture of me on Facebook.

After lunch, the boys had gone out for a walk and Tim and I were sitting in the garden having a relaxing coffee and reading the newspapers. It was time for me to open up to Tim about my one-night-stand ten years ago. I could feel my heart beating fast and I was so nervous but I needed to do this. I took a deep breath and turned towards him.

"Tim, there's been something on my mind that I need to talk to you about, something that I should have told you ten years ago. I did something very stupid and I'm so ashamed of myself, but I need to tell you about it."

Tim turned towards me and reached out, putting his hand over my arm. I bit my lip trying to hold myself together as he spoke.

"Ten years ago, was a very difficult time for you Libby, you held this family together single-handedly. I was very lucky not to have lost you and I am so grateful that you stood by me."

I started to interrupt him, to tell him that I needed to explain something to him, but he squeezed my arm and looked directly into my eyes saying in his gentle way:

"Libby, whatever you think you have to tell me, whatever you think you are ashamed of, it's nothing compared to what I've felt of myself in the past and what I've put you through, so if it was ten years ago, then we should be drawing a line under it and we should forget about it. No good can come of raking over the past. We love each other, don't we?"

I nodded, tears threatening to prickle behind my eyes, I bit my lip again.

"Well, that's all that matters, just you and me and the boys, nothing else, everything from the past is just the past and nothing more."

I nodded again, "I think I'm very lucky to have you Dr Ashford."

"And I'm very happy to have you Mrs Ashford."

Just then a magpie landed on the grass, I glanced at Tim and said, "One for sorrow?"

"Two for Joy," he smiled and nodded over towards the other side of the garden where the magpie's mate was sitting.

We were quiet for a little while then Tim mused, "I'm sure there was a children's TV programme that had a song about magpies, but I can't remember what it was."

"It was just called *Magpie,* but it was on at the same time as *Blue Peter* and a similar programme, so I didn't often watch it. What made you think of that?"

"I've been trying to remember the rest of the song from the theme tune. I know it started:

One for Sorrow,

Two for Joy.

but I can't for the life of me remember any of the rest."

"You're right, I think the next lines are:

*Three for a Girl,*
*Four for a Boy"*

"Yes, that's it," Tim said distractedly and immediately went back to his crossword.

We sat companionably reading in silence but I was still thinking about the theme tune, and then the lines came to me.

*One for sorrow,*
*Two for Joy,*
*Three for a Girl,*
*Four for a Boy,*
*Five for Silver,*
*Six for Gold,*
*Seven for a Secret, Never to be told.*

I looked at Tim wondering if he had remembered any more lines of the song too, but he was engrossed in his crossword. It crossed my mind that he had been trying to tell me something, but I don't think he would be so cryptic, he would just come right out and say it surely?

I felt suddenly weary with a heaviness in my heart and a sadness that I felt I would carry forever, because despite Tim drawing a line under everything and telling me that nothing else mattered, it felt like a heavy chain had been wrapped around my heart. I knew now that I would always have my guilty secret to keep and that I would always be looking over my shoulder, worrying that someday, out of nowhere, my secret might come back to haunt me.

Because no good can ever come of having secrets.

## The End

# Author's Notes

Whilst Cranachlove House is a fictional house, it is loosely based on an ancient House in East Lothian: Lennoxlove House.

Lennoxlove House is a historic house set in woodlands half a mile south of Haddington in East Lothian. Described by *Historic Scotland* as one of Scotland's most ancient and notable houses, it comprises a 15$^{th}$ century tower and has been extended several times and protected as a category a listed building. It is now the seat of the Duke of Hamilton and Brandon.

Whilst there is no Charity Shield Cricket match held with 'the locals' every year, Haddington does have a Cricket Club which is the oldest cricket club in East Lothian, Founded in 1877.

The cricket match was used initially because I needed a mechanism to bring Tim's nickname into the story, and as with many groups and institutions, sports clubs do tend to favour nicknames, regardless of what the individual who is given the nickname feels.

In the section about the cricket match, we first hear from Libby who sits literally on the outside of the boundary, she is gradually drawn into the game and into what is happening, guided by the old gentleman. She knows nothing of what is going on initially.

Tim, who we hear from next is experiencing everything from within the game. It is at this point that he is starting to disclose something, a deep, shameful and hurtful secret from his past that he has been trying to forget.

At the stage in their relationship, Tim and Libby are still strangers, it is Grandpa/Phillip that is the link between the two characters, telling Libby that Tim has a story to tell.

If there are any cricket fans reading the story, they may pick up the fact that what Libby sees during the match is actually an exact mirror of what Tim is experiencing. In her chapter, a number of overs are described in detail: a dot ball; a maiden over; a googley etc., (as is explained by Phillip, the old gentleman). But in Tim's chapter, he is living the very same experience, the 'no run' (dot ball); the maiden over (they just can't get them out); the wicket taken by the googley etc. It is a way of showing that Libby sees things from Tim's world but that his experiences go deeper.

The game of cricket in the story is quite symbolic of the two characters, Libby on the outside looking at Tim, and Tim experiencing the pain from within. It is symbolic because there are other points in the story where Tim withdraws into himself and Libby is left on the outside looking in, trying to fathom what is going on in his world. Of course, at the point of the cricket match, we don't know this yet.

The cricket terminology may be a bit off putting, but to a certain extent, it can be brushed over, it's only a couple of pages really! In reality, you could spend five days watching a cricket test match only for the match to be drawn at the end!

If you are ever in the Highlands in the Rothiemurchas, Alvie and Kincraig area, you will indeed find the Kincraig Art Café selling amazing cakes and Italian street food, wine, bottled beers and coffee. The Art Café is also a gallery for original artwork of Ann Vastano, and prints of the local area where you will find beautiful and dramatic images of places mentioned in the book including Ben Macdui, Corrour Bothy and Ryvoan Bothy.